James Hadley Chase and The Murder Room

〉〉〉 This title is part of The Murder Room, our series dedicated to making available out-of-print or hard-to-find titles by classic crime writers.

Crime fiction has always held up a mirror to society. The Victorians were fascinated by sensational murder and the emerging science of detection; now we are obsessed with the forensic detail of violent death. And no other genre has so captivated and enthralled readers.

Vast troves of classic crime writing have for a long time been unavailable to all but the most dedicated frequenters of second-hand bookshops. The advent of digital publishing means that we are now able to bring you the backlists of a huge range of titles by classic and contemporary crime writers, some of which have been out of print for decades.

From the genteel amateur private eyes of the Golden Age and the femmes fatales of pulp fiction, to the morally ambiguous hard-boiled detectives of mid twentieth-century America and their descendants who walk our twenty-first century streets, The Murder Room has it all. 〉〉〉

The Murder Room
Where Criminal Minds Meet

themurderroom.com

James Hadley Chase (1906–1985)

Born René Brabazon Raymond in London, the son of a British colonel in the Indian Army, James Hadley Chase was educated at King's School in Rochester, Kent, and left home at the age of 18. He initially worked in book sales until, inspired by the rise of gangster culture during the Depression and by reading James M. Cain's *The Postman Always Rings Twice*, he wrote his first novel, *No Orchids for Miss Blandish*. Despite the American setting of many of his novels, Chase (like Peter Cheyney, another hugely successful British noir writer) never lived there, writing with the aid of maps and a slang dictionary. He had phenomenal success with the novel, which continued unabated throughout his entire career, spanning 45 years and nearly 90 novels. His work was published in dozens of languages and over thirty titles were adapted for film. He served in the RAF during World War II, where he also edited the RAF Journal. In 1956 he moved to France with his wife and son; they later moved to Switzerland, where Chase lived until his death in 1985.

By James Hadley Chase
(published in The Murder Room)

The Joker in the Pack

James Hadley Chase

An Orion book

Copyright © Hervey Raymond 1975

The right of James Hadley Chase to be identified as the author of this
work has been asserted in accordance with the Copyright, Designs and
Patents Act 1988.

This edition published by
The Orion Publishing Group Ltd
Orion House
5 Upper St Martin's Lane
London WC2H 9EA

An Hachette UK company
A CIP catalogue record for this book is available from the British Library

ISBN 978 1 4719 0388 5

www.orionbooks.co.uk

This one is for David Higham,
a good and wise friend for over thirty years

CHAPTER ONE

THE Zurich–Miami Jumbo touched down at the Miami International airport at 10.35, according to schedule.

Usually Helga Rolfe enjoyed travelling V.I.P., cosseted and pampered as the wife of one of the world's richest men, fawned over by young air hostesses, receiving a visit from the flight captain, but this time the flight had been irksome and the V.I.P. treatment irritating, for Helga had a problem on her mind, such a problem she would have welcomed solitude, welcomed not having to make brittle conversation with the flight captain who was very aware of his sexuality and who leaned over her, touching his massive moustache while he oozed charm.

It was a relief to leave the plane, to be conveyed in a Cadillac across the runway to the Miami–Nassau plane, knowing her luggage would follow, that she would be taken care of by a young eager air hostess who would guide her to her seat for the last leg of the journey where her crippled husband, Herman Rolfe, would be waiting.

Because of the power and the magic of Rolfe's name, she was first on board with the adjacent seat vacant. Already the steward was at her side, minutes before the other passengers were finding their seats, with a bottle of champagne which Helga didn't refuse. She asked for a dash of cognac. She felt in need of a stimulant after the wearingly long flight across the Atlantic.

As the plane took off, she leaned her head back against the rest, her active mind busy. During the long flight from Zurich she had gone through the accounts and had satisfied herself there were two million dollars missing. Archer had admitted this. Actually it was $2,150,000, but near enough. She wondered how Herman would react when she told him he'd been swindled. Certainly he would alert his New York

1

lawyers who would descend on Archer like a wolf pack. That was inevitable, but how would Herman react to her involvement? This worried her. Would he regard her as a dupe or an innocent or a fool – even worse, someone he could no longer trust?

She allowed the steward to re-fill her glass. The champagne and brandy, well mixed, was relaxing. She thought of those nightmare days and nights in the Swiss villa at Castagnola with Archer, held prisoner, and that stupid, but well meaning homosexual who she had hoped would have been a lover.* Thinking of him, the sexual urge that always tormented her, swept through her body. There was a youngish man, handsome and well built, sitting across the aisle, reading *Time*. She looked swiftly at him, then away. A man, she told herself, who would be interesting in bed. She closed her eyes. These thoughts, she warned herself must be banished. She was returning to her husband, crippled, sexually useless, but dangerously suspicious.

'Mrs. Rolfe . . .'

The young air hostess was beside her, blue shaded eyelids, long eye lashes fluttering.

Helga glanced up, frowning.

These young girls, she told herself bitterly, had no problems. When the sex urge hit them they surrendered to it. They had nothing to conceal as she had: nothing to fear. They went to some motel or hotel – anywhere. For them sex presented no complications.

'Yes?'

'We land in ten minutes, Mrs. Rolfe. Please fasten your safety belt.'

As a V.I.P. she was first off the plane to find Hinkle waiting on the tarmac with the two toned Silver Shadow Rolls.

Hinkle, looking like a well fed, benign English bishop and who acted as Rolfe's nurse, valet and chef, had at first frightened Helga. He was and always would be a perfectionist. Rotund, bald, with white wisps of hair to soften his florid complexion, Hinkle, although looking older than his fifty years, was surprisingly athletic and strong. When she had married Herman, Hinkle seemed ready to disapprove but

* See 'Ace up my Sleeve.'

2

after some six months, after watching her closely, he seemed to accept that she was also a perfectionist, clever, nimble minded and a professional. Although he remained aloof, the perfect servant, she now had the feeling that he not only approved of her, but even admired her.

'I trust you had a good journey, madame,' he said in his fruity, clerical voice.

'It was all right.' She walked towards the Rolls with quick, graceful strides. Hinkle kept pace with her, slightly behind her. 'How is Mr. Rolfe?'

'You will see, madame.' Hinkle was now ahead of her to open the off-side door. She paused to look back. The man who had been reading *Time* was walking towards the arrival gate. Again she became aware of this wearisome but compelling sexual urge. She sank into the leather upholstery while Hinkle slid under the driving wheel.

The Silver Cloud made its silent way from the airport. Officials saluted her. Her reception would have pleased the wife of the President, she thought. Rolfe's power and magic at times could be burdensome, but at other times, a magic key that unlocked the doors of the world.

'Isn't he well?' she asked.

'No, madame. The journey seems to have been a strain. He has been working extremely hard. Dr. Levi flew in this morning. He is with him now.'

She stiffened. 'Is he bad?'

'Let us say poorly,' Hinkle returned. He never committed himself to outright statements. 'Poorly' could even mean that Herman was dying.

Knowing Hinkle, Helga shifted ground.

'And the hotel?'

'You will see, madame. It is most unfortunate that there are no suitable villas to hire. Mr. Rolfe made an impulsive decision to come here. He was disappointed not to go to Switzerland. Had he given me a week's notice, I could have arranged something.' Hinkle's fruity voice lowered a tone: his way of conveying his vexation. She knew how he hated hotel life where he couldn't cook, fuss nor supervise.

'Isn't there anywhere?'

'Apparently not, madame.'

3

'Does Mr. Rolfe intend to stay long at the hotel?'

Hinkle drove along the wide road which ran by the magnificent beach with its palms, its bathers, its emerald green sea.

'That, I think, madame, will depend on Dr. Levi.'

They arrived at the opulent Diamond Beach hotel with its championship tennis courts, its pitch and putt golf, its vast pool and its private beach.

Two flunkeys were waiting. Helga walked into the ornate lobby to be met by the manager who bowed as he shook hands. She was hot and tired, wearing the wrong clothes, coming straight from Zurich, snow bound and icy. She was whisked to the top floor and after polite inquiries about a drink, a suggestion of lunch served on the terrace, much bowing, she was left alone.

She threw off her clothes and went into the bathroom. A tepid, scented bath had already been drawn. Naked, she paused in front of the ceiling to floor mirror.

She was wearing well, she told herself in spite of her forty-three years. She was slim, flat bellied, heavy breasted, rounded hips. Her face? She examined it, leaning forward, frowning. Tired, of course. Who wouldn't be tired after that goddam flight? Tired, but interesting. High cheek bones, large violet coloured eyes, a short, beautifully shaped nose, full lips and a perfect complexion. Yes ... the glamour remained in spite of the years.

When she had bathed, she put on a cotton trouser suit. Her personal maid, Maria, had sent her all the necessary Nassau clothes. Feeling more relaxed, she called room service.

'A double vodka martini and smoked salmon sandwiches,' she ordered.

She went out on to the terrace and looked down at the distant beach. Men, women; boys and girls, all shapes and sizes, were baking themselves in the brilliant sun. The sea lapped the sand. Girls squealed. Boys chased. Again Helga felt this frustrating sexual urge. She went back into the cool of the living room and picking up the telephone receiver asked if Dr. Levi was in the hotel. An anonymous, servile voice said he was and please hold a moment, Mrs. Rolfe.

Dr. Levi came on the line after a brief delay. He had a

soft, soothing voice and was always deferential as if addressing royalty when he spoke to her.

'So happy to hear you arrived safely, Mrs. Rolfe,' he said. 'You must be exhausted. Can I do anything? A tranquillizer, perhaps?'

She knew him to be the most expensive and most brilliant doctor in Paradise City and she knew he was enormously rich and his deference to the name of Rolfe irritated her.

'Could you come up, doctor?'

'Of course.'

He arrived soon after the waiter had brought the smoked salmon sandwiches and a shaker of vodka martini.

'A drink, doctor?' she asked.

'Thank you, no. But sit down, Mrs. Rolfe. You have had ...'

'Yes.' As she sat down, she looked at him: a tiny, bird-like man with a hooked nose, rimless glasses, a dome of a forehead. 'Tell me about my husband.'

Dr. Levi sat down. He, like her, was a professional. He, like her, spoke directly.

'Mr. Rolfe is sixty-eight,' he said quietly. 'He insists on working at a tremendous pressure. At his age and in his condition, it is time to call a halt: for him to relax and to give what remains of his body a chance to recuperate, but Mr. Rolfe continues to drive himself. For the past three weeks he has been setting up a deal that would test the fittest of men, let alone an elderly cripple. Now he flies from New York to here.' Dr. Levi paused and shrugged. 'The fact is, Mrs. Rolfe, your husband is in very poor shape but refuses to admit it. My advice to him is to return to the comforts of his home and cut off all work and do nothing except laze in the sun for at least three months.'

Helga reached for another sandwich.

'No one has ever been able to stop him working.'

Dr. Levi nodded.

'Yes. That is why I am leaving this afternoon. I have less important patients to look after, but more deserving. They will accept my advice whereas your husband won't. I am speaking in strict confidence. If your husband continues to work as he is doing, he will die.'

5

'So long as he is happy ... does it really matter?' Helga asked.

Dr. Levi stared at her, then nodded.

'There is that. Yes, when one reaches his age, is in continual pain and crippled, then I suppose ...' He spread his hands.

'As his wife I am concerned. Will you please be frank with me? Can he last long?' She realized as soon as she had said this that she had been voicing her secret thoughts and regretted what she had said, but Dr. Levi appeared to understand.

'He could die tomorrow. He could die next year. Give and take, I would say perhaps he has six months in which to live unless he gives up working and completely relaxes.'

'But he is relaxing now, doctor.'

'No. He is constantly on the telephone. He is constantly getting telegrams, cables, telex messages and so on. Even here, he is directing his empire.'

'This is something neither you nor I can do anything about.'

'That is correct. I have warned him. He brushes my advice aside so, this afternoon I am returning to Paradise City.'

When he had gone, she thoughtfully finished the sandwiches. She drank another vodka martini. When Herman dies, she thought, I will inherit sixty million dollars and I will be free to do just what I like. I can have any man I want ... when he dies!

Slightly drunk, feeling confident, she telephoned Hinkle.

'Does Mr. Rolfe know I have arrived?'

'Yes, madame. He is expecting you. It is the third door on the left as you leave your apartment.'

She went to the mirror and regarded herself. Herman was very critical about a woman's appearance. Satisfied, she picked up the leather portfolio containing the damning accounts and bracing herself, she left the room.

She found her husband in his wheel chair, in the full glare of the sun. The vast terrace, its view, the sun umbrellas, the boxes of gay flowers and the bar were all symbols of his power and wealth.

As she crossed the terrace, she looked at him: an alarmingly thin body, balding head, thin pinched nostrils, lipless mouth. The black sun goggles made her think of a dressed up skull.

'Ah, Helga . . .' His usual cold greeting.

'Well . . .' she sat down fairly close to him but in the shade of an umbrella. She found the Nassau sun, after the Swiss sun, a little overpowering.

They spoke trivialities: she inquiring about his health, he inquiring, without interest, about her flight. He told her he wasn't feeling too well, but that fool Levi always made a mountain out of a molehill. Neither of them believed what he said.

After this empty skirmishing, he said abruptly, 'You have something to tell me?'

'Yes.' She braced herself. 'Jack Archer has turned out to be an embezzler and a forger.'

She looked directly at him, expecting an explosion, but there was no change of expression. How she wished there had been! If he had even stiffened, changed colour, she would feel he was human, but the skull-like face remained skull-like.

'I know that.' His voice was harsh. 'Two million.'

A chill crept up her spine.

'How can you possibly know?'

'Know? It is my business to know! Have you imagined that I don't check on everything that concerns my money?' He raised a thin hand. 'Archer stole intelligently. Mobile. Transalpine. Nacional Financial. Chevron. Calcomp. Hobart and General Motors. At least, thief as he is, he showed intelligence.'

When he had tried to blackmail her, Archer had assured her that Rolfe wouldn't know what bonds, what shares he had stolen. He had told her that Rolfe's portfolio was so vast he wouldn't miss the certificates and she had believed him. Crushed, she sat silent, looking down at the leather portfolio that now contained no secrets.

'So Archer is a forger and an embezzler,' Rolfe went on. 'It happens. I misjudged the man. I take it he forged your signature?'

Feeling utterly defeated, Helga said, 'Yes.'

'I should have thought of that possibility. There should have been a third signature. We will write this off as an experience.'

She stared at him bewildered. 'But you will prosecute him?'

His head turned. The black goggles were directed at her.

'Fortunately, I can afford not to prosecute. Two million? To many it is a large sum but fortunately to me, it isn't. Of course, I have already arranged that Archer will never ever get a responsible job again. He will find life much harder and more depressing than serving a term in jail. From now on, no one will touch Archer. He will join the ranks of the shifty, the shoddy and the fringe people.'

Helga sat motionless, her heart beating unevenly, sure that there was more behind this act of so called mercy ... not to prosecute.

Finally, she said, 'I was sure you would prosecute.'

He nodded.

'I would have prosecuted but for one thing.' His head turned, the goggles pointed away from her. 'I have been informed that before our marriage you were Archer's mistress. I have been advised that if I prosecute Archer, this sordid fact will become public. Archer could sully you in court. I am prepared to forgo the satisfaction of jailing him to protect you and myself from scandal.'

Her mind went back to that moment when he had asked her to marry him.

He had asked, 'Does sex mean a lot to you?' Then he had gone on, 'I am a cripple. I am asking you if you are prepared to give up a normal sex life to become my wife. When we marry there must never be any other man ... never a breath of scandal. That is something I will not tolerate. If you cheat, Helga, I will divorce you and you will be left with nothing. Remember that. If you remain faithful to me, I will give you a fulfilled life. There are many compensations which I have discovered that can replace sex. If you are prepared to accept this condition then we can be married as soon as I can make the arrangements.'

She had agreed to his terms, believing then that sex could

be replaced by the advantages and the glamour of being the wife of one of the world's richest men, but it hadn't worked out like that. To her, she had to accept the fact that sex was life.

'I am sorry,' was all she could find to say.

He shrugged.

'That is all right. The past is the past.' Rolfe moved restlessly. 'I am relieving you of the burden of handling my money, Helga. I now only expect you to act as my hostess; continue to enjoy my money and remain a faithful wife. Winborn will take over the Swiss portfolio.' He dug a thin finger into the bell push at his side.

Shocked, suddenly furious, Helga said, 'So you no longer trust me?'

'It is not a matter of trust,' Rolfe said, his voice hard and cold. 'Of course you are not to blame. Rather I am to blame for choosing Archer. You have done very well. I have been satisfied, but it is better, under the circumstances to relieve you of further responsibilities.'

Hinkle came out on to the terrace in answer to the bell. Seeing them, he paused discreetly, out of hearing.

Helga said angrily, 'So I am to be downgraded ... punished because of your own stupid judgement!'

The black goggles swung in her direction. The skull-like face remained impassive.

'Enjoy the beach, Helga.' Rolfe's voice revealed his complete indifference. 'And behave yourself. Remember this ... I seldom make a mistake, but when I do, I never repeat it.'

He snapped his thin fingers at Hinkle who came forward.

Leaving the portfolio on the chair, Helga, flushed and furious, left the terrace and returned to her apartment.

The only child of a brilliant international lawyer, Helga had had a continental education. She had had training in law and secretarial practice. Her father had joined a firm in Lausanne, Switzerland, specializing in tax problems. When she was twenty-four and fully qualified, her father had brought her into the firm as his personal assistant. She had a flair for finance and quickly made herself indispensable. The heart attack that killed her father some six years later made no difference to her position with the firm. Jack Archer, one of the junior partners, grabbed her as his personal secretary. He was handsome, dynamic and magnificently sexy. She had always been over-sexed. Men were necessary in her life and she had so many lovers she had lost count of them. She became Archer's mistress an hour or so after she had agreed to work with him. Somehow, no one seemed to know quite how, Archer got hold of the Herman Rolfe account and by doing so became a senior partner. Helga had helped him handle the massive portfolio. Rolfe had been impressed by her financial flair, her looks and her personality. He had offered marriage. Urged on by Archer, she had accepted. All had gone well until Archer had been tempted to make himself a quick million dollars by investing in Australian nickel where there was no nickel. To save himself, he had forged Helga's signature and had taken over two million dollars of Rolfe's money.

Sitting on the terrace, staring out at the beach, Helga heard again Archer's persuasive words: 'Look Helga, Herman needn't know about this. You know he never checks anything. He is far too busy. You initial all this stuff and he accepts it. I'm asking you to help me out of a hole. After all he's worth around sixty million ... he will never miss two, will he?'

Although she was sure Herman wouldn't miss two million, she had refused to be Archer's accomplice. How right she had been! For Herman knew that Archer had turned embezzler before she could tell him! She drew in a long, deep breath. Thank God, she hadn't submitted to Archer's attempted blackmail!

So ...

It is better, under the circumstances, to relieve you of further responsibilities.

The crippled bastard! After all she had done for him! After all the money she had made for him by shrewd and careful investing! To be tossed aside like this!

I now only expect you to be my hostess; continue to enjoy my money and remain a faithful wife.

No longer would she have the excuse to fly to Lausanne, Paris, Bonn, representing him. No longer would she receive the V.I.P. treatment at the airports and the luxury hotels. A hostess! A smiling face, the right words to fat, old men who wanted favours from her husband, who fawned over her, hoping she might advance their interests. No more freedom! No more waiters who came to her room, serviced her and went away with money in their experienced hands. No more young, well-built men, ready and willing. It was only on her travels that she looked for lovers: never in Miami, Paradise City, New York: Herman's neck of the woods. She was now condemned to sit in this kind of hotel or in the luxury of the Paradise City villa or in the New York penthouse with her crippled husband always nearby, staring at her behind black sun goggles.

Then she thought of what Dr. Levi had said. *He could die tomorrow. He could die next year. Give and take, I would say perhaps six months unless he gives up this rat race and relaxes.*

That Herman would never do. So ... six months! She was prepared to wait six months. And then ...! Sixty million dollars! Rolfe's magic key her own!

She put on a bikini swim suit. Still not entirely sure of herself, she again surveyed herself in the mirror. The Swiss winter tan was becoming but paling a little. Her figure was provocative. She knew this. Pulling on a beach wrap, she took the elevator to the lobby.

The reception manager was immediately at her side.

'Is there anything, madame?'

'Yes, please ... a beach buggy.'

'Of course.'

No more than a three minute wait and the beach buggy was pulling up at the hotel entrance. The smiling attendant offered to show her the controls, but she was familiar with the controls of machines on wheels.

A smiling traffic cop, obviously alerted, stopped the traffic and gave her a salute as she drove across the main road and on to the beach. She waved to him, smiling. A beautiful man, she thought. God! How I would like him in my bed!

Driving fast, she soon put the crowds behind her and headed for the sand dunes, the deserted beach and the sea. When she was sure she was on her own, she left the beach buggy and throwing off her wrap, she ran into the sea. She swam furiously, getting rid of all that irked her: Herman, Archer, her boxed-in future. She was an excellent swimmer, and by swimming fast, she came out of the water feeling cleansed both in mind and body.

As she walked back to the beach buggy, her step faltered. A man in swim trunks was standing by the vehicle, examining it: a big man with muscular shoulders, deeply-tanned body, black, over long hair and green sun goggles.

He looked towards her and grinned, showing big white teeth, teeth good enough to feature on a T.V. commercial. In spite of the sun goggles which hid his eyes; the rest of his face was friendly, pleasant without being handsome.

'Hi, there,' he said, 'I was admiring this thing. Is it yours?'

'It belongs to the hotel,' Helga said and reached for her wrap. He got it before she did and with just the right movements, nothing familiar, nothing servile, he helped her on with it. 'Thank you.'

'I'm Harry Jackson,' he told her. 'Down here on vacation. I saw you swimming. Olympic style,' and he grinned.

She looked sharply at him, but he wasn't putting her on. He had said what he meant.

'Well ...' She shrugged, pleased. 'I swim a bit. Are you enjoying your vacation, Mr. Jackson?'

'I sure am. This is the first time I have visited this neck of the woods. It's something, isn't it?'

'It would seem so. I have only just arrived.'

'I want to do some skin diving. Do you skin dive?'

'Yes.' What didn't she do? she wondered.

'Would you know the best place ... no, I guess that's a stupid question ... you just arriving.'

She had been studying him, his beautiful muscles, his frank smile, his sexuality and that crucifying sex urge boiled up in her. If he had grabbed and raped her, it would have been the moment of her life. She looked up and down the deserted beach. They were utterly alone.

There was a pause, then she said. 'How did you get here?'

'Oh, I walked. I like walking.' He smiled. 'I got tired of all the noise. People sure know how to enjoy themselves here but they kick up a hell of a racket.'

'Yes.' She moved to the beach buggy and got in. 'Do you want a ride back?'

'Thanks. I've had all the walking I want for today.' He climbed in beside her.

As she started the engine, she looked more closely at him. He was probably thirty-three, not more: ten years her junior, she thought. She wished he would take off the sun goggles. A man's eyes, to her, were important.

'What do you do for a living, Mr. Jackson?' she asked. She wanted to know into what class category she would place him.

'I'm a salesman,' Jackson said. 'I travel around. I like the life. I'm free . . . on my own. That's important to me.'

And to me too, Helga thought as she set the buggy in motion.

'What do you sell?'

'Kitchen equipment.'

'That's good, isn't it? Everyone needs kitchen equipment.' She was thinking: small fry, not dangerous, no connections with any of Herman's awful people . . . he could be safe.

'Right. I enjoy it. As you say, people always need something for the kitchen.'

'Where are you staying, Mr. Jackson?'

'I've rented a beach hut. I look after myself. I like it that way. Hotels give me a pain.'

'Yes. Does your wife like that way of life?'

He laughed: an easy lilting laugh.

'I haven't a wife, I like my freedom. I haven't even a girl friend here, but I'll find someone. I believe in ships that pass in the night . . . no complications,' and he laughed again.

She very nearly stopped the buggy and told him to take her, but she controlled herself.

'I'm Helga,' she said. 'I'm on my own tonight. Should we do something about it?'

Was he going to duck out? Was he going to tell her by a look, not in words that she was too old for him. Her fingers turned white on the driving wheel.

'Wonderful!' He sounded enthusiastic. 'Let's do that. Where and when do I pick you up?'

13

'Have you a car?'

'Sure.'

'Then why not outside the Ocean Beach club at nine o'clock?'

She had seen the club some hundred yards down the road from her hotel. At nine o'clock, Herman would be in bed.

'It's a date. I look forward to it.' He thought for a moment. 'There's a sea food restaurant I know. Do you like sea food?'

'Of course.'

'Fine. It's okay ... you don't have to dress. Anything goes. Right?'

'Yes.'

They drove for some minutes in silence, then he said, 'Helga ... that's an unusual name.' He suddenly took off his sun goggles and smiled at her. His big, friendly eyes gave her confidence. He was all right, she told herself. No problem with him. 'You're unusual too.'

She laughed, delighted.

'We will talk about that tonight?'

'That's my beach hut.' He pointed. They were about half a mile from her hotel.

She slowed the buggy, looked at the line of huts standing a hundred yards or so from the sea, half hidden by palm trees. She stopped the buggy.

'Well, then tonight at nine,' she said.

'Right.' He put his hand lightly but possessively on her arm for a brief moment. His touch sent a shock through her. He knew what she wanted, she told herself. 'See you and thanks for the ride.'

In an excited daze, she drove back to the hotel.

The time was 19.15. Alex, the amiable hotel hairdresser had done her hair: his assistant had given her a facial. A waiter had brought her a shaker of vodka martinis. She had had a nap and was now refreshed and thinking of her date at 21.00 at the Ocean Beach club.

She had put on a simple white dress: white was becoming. It showed up her tan and, looking at herself in the mirror, she was satisfied. She would have one more drink, then she would go along to say good night to Herman, telling him she intended to take a walk, needing to stretch her legs after the journey. He wouldn't be interested, but she would tell him.

As she poured the drink, the telephone bell buzzed. Frowning, she lifted the receiver.

'Do I disturb you, madame?'

She recognized Hinkle's fruity voice.

Surprised, she said, 'Why no, Hinkle. What is it?'

'If you could spare me a few minutes, madame?'

'Of course.'

'Thank you, madame,' and he hung up.

Puzzled, Helga sat down, sipped her drink and waited. She couldn't imagine what Hinkle wanted to see her about unless it was about Herman. She had known Hinkle now for some three years. He had never approached her in this way before and she had seldom asked him to do anything for her. She had her own personal maid, and she regarded Hinkle strictly as Herman's property.

A light tap came on the door and Hinkle entered. He was wearing a white jacket, a black bow tie and black trousers. In spite of the servant's uniform, he still looked like a benign bishop.

He shut the door, moved further into the room, then paused.

She looked inquiringly at him.

'Yes, Hinkle?'

'I would like, madame, if you would permit, to speak frankly with you.'

'Is it about Mr. Rolfe?'

'Yes, madame.'

'Won't you sit down?'

'Thank you, madame. I would rather not.' A pause, then he went on, 'I have worked for Mr. Rolfe for some fifteen years. He is not an easy gentleman to work for but I believe I have given him acceptable service.'

'I know you have, Hinkle,' Helga said quickly. Was he breaking the news that he had had enough of Herman and was leaving? She shrank from the thought. 'No one could have done more for him.'

'I believe that is so, madame. I now find myself in a

15

distressing position. Naturally, after all these years, I have a feeling of loyalty to Mr. Rolfe. As you know I look after Mr. Rolfe's papers when he is travelling. Mr. Rolfe has come to regard me as a background figure: someone who is always at hand, someone who is neuter if you follow my meaning. While filing some papers I came across a draft letter to Mr. Winborn. In order to place it where Mr. Rolfe could find it again, I read it. I now find myself in a dilemma. However, there was a subsequent happening and I decided I must speak to you.'

Helga stiffened.

'I don't know what you mean,' she said sharply.

'If you will bear with me, madame, I will explain as you have given me permission to speak frankly.'

'Well?'

'I have to admit, to my regret, that I did not approve of you when you married Mr. Rolfe. Since I have got to know you, madame, I have come to realize your worth, what you have done for Mr. Rolfe, the burden you have accepted to make his home life easy, your constant journeys on his behalf. If I may say so, madame, I am impressed by your industry, your unfailing willingness, your financial abilities and the sacrifices you have made.'

Helga sat back, staring.

'Well, Hinkle, that is quite a testimonial. Thank you.'

'I don't speak lightly on such matters, madame,' Hinkle said, looking directly at her. 'Mr. Rolfe is far from well. I realize this more than Dr. Levi does since I am in such close contact with Mr. Rolfe. I have discerned a distressing mental weakness in Mr. Rolfe which Dr. Levi, so far, has failed to observe.'

'You mean my husband's mind is deteriorating?' This was the last thing Helga expected to hear.

'Not quite that, madame. Mr. Rolfe suffers a great deal. Probably due to the drugs that Dr. Levi prescribes he appears now to be developing an odd persecution mania.'

Helga experienced a little jolt.

'What makes you say that?'

'I find this difficult to tell you, madame.' Hinkle looked distressed. 'For some time, Mr. Rolfe has spoken to me of

16

you with kindness, respect and even admiration. His attitude, recently, appears to have changed.'

Startled, Helga said, 'It has?'

'Yes, madame. He also appears to be taking a sudden interest in his daughter, Miss Sheila. You may perhaps know that Mr. Rolfe and she quarrelled. She left home, and for the past three years, has not communicated with him.'

'I heard something about it,' Helga said tensely.

'This draft letter to Mr. Winborn, madame, gives Mr. Winborn instructions about a new will. What Mr. Rolfe does with his money is no concern of mine. However, in view of your constant attention to Mr. Rolfe and in view of a subsequent happening, I felt you should be forewarned.'

'What subsequent happening?' Helga was aware that her voice had turned husky.

'I regret to tell you, madame, that I overheard Mr. Rolfe on the telephone yesterday giving instructions to a private inquiry agency to have you watched. Knowing you are deserving of Mr. Rolfe's trust, I consider this so disgraceful I can only assume that Mr. Rolfe has become mentally ill.'

A private inquiry agency! Helga turned cold. She stared down at her hands while she struggled to absorb the shock.

'Mr. Rolfe is now in bed,' Hinkle said, slightly lowering his voice. 'I have given him a sedative. The draft letter to Mr. Winborn which I think you should see is in the lower right hand drawer of his desk. It has yet to be mailed.'

She looked up.

'Thank you, Hinkle.'

He moved towards the door.

'There is such a thing as justice, madame,' and he left the room.

After some fifteen years of the ruthless cut-and-thrust of modern business, Helga had acquired the capacity of weathering shocks, disasters, and even catastrophies, and she had experienced a few. She now absorbed this shock quickly. Cold fury gripped her as her shrewd brain went into action. How had Herman become suspicious? She didn't believe for a moment Hinkle's theory that Herman was mentally ill. Had he heard some gossip? Had he received an anonymous letter? She had been so careful in her sexual adventures. She thought of Hinkle. *Knowing you are deserving of Mr. Rolfe's trust.* Kind, nice minded Hinkle! She finished her drink, then lit a cigarette. To be watched by some sleazy investigator! But that wasn't the immediate problem. Herman had written a letter, changing his will, to Stanley Winborn, the head of his legal department: a tall, forbidding stick of a man whom she hated, who she knew strongly disapproved of her marriage and who had been nearly ill with jealousy when Rolfe had given Archer his Swiss portfolio.

She must know what she was facing. She must see this letter. Forewarned was forearmed. She recalled her father's cliché. Without hesitating, she stubbed out her cigarette and made her way to Herman's suite. Entering the living room, she moved silently to the bedroom. The door stood ajar. She looked in. Herman lay motionless. A soft light cast a glimmer on the worn, hard face. The eyes, usually hidden behind the big black goggles were closed. She felt a tremor run through her. Except for the slight rise and fall of the sheets covering him, he could have been dead.

Softly, she said, 'Herman?'

He didn't move.

Turning, she went silently to the big desk that stood in the bay window. Opening the lower right hand drawer, she found a red leather folder. Placing it on the desk, she switched on the shaded lamp.

Her heart was beating unevenly as she opened the folder. There was the letter:

My dear Winborn.

The writing was small, neat and easy to read. Her eyes raced along the lines.

Re my will.

I have reason to believe that Helga is no longer fit nor deserving to inherit my fortune nor to handle my Swiss portfolio. In spite of your advice which I now regret ignoring, I made a will (in your keeping and which must be destroyed on receipt of this letter) giving her complete control of some sixty million dollars. When I made this will Helga had so impressed me with her honesty and financial acumen that I had complete confidence in her to continue to administer my money as I have administered it. However, I now learn that she has allowed Archer to swindle me out of two million dollars and even worse, have evidence, admittedly flimsy, that she has been misbehaving herself while in Europe. When I married her, I warned her I would not tolerate any scandal. So disturbing is this evidence, I have arranged to have her watched by a competent inquiry agency. Should 'hard' evidence be obtained, I will immediately divorce her.

As my executor, I want you, together with Frederick Loman, to take over control of my Swiss portfolio. I attach a revised list of bequests. As I am satisfied that Helga has betrayed my trust and that she has been associating with various men without, so far, giving me tangible proof, I have decided, at my death, that she is only to receive a tax free income of one hundred thousand dollars a year subject to the following conditions: she is to create no scandal, she is not to marry again and she is to be subjected to a snap check from time to time by a competent inquiry agency that she is behaving herself. She is to have no access to capital: she is only to receive income. She may have the use of all my houses, villas and apartments and you will supervise the accounts. She is to lose these privileges and her income if she contravenes the above conditions.

I often wonder about my daughter, Sheila. She has been a great worry to me but she did have the integrity to assume another name (which I do not know) so that her radical political interests and her distressing way of life have never sullied the Rolfe name. As a reward for this, I wish to leave her one million dollars.

Please put all these points in legal shape and send me the draft at your earliest.

Regards,
  Herman Rolfe.

For some moments, Helga sat staring at the letter. Her first reaction was bitter despair: not to marrry again! No more affairs! The old devil was condemning her to the life of a nun! How Winborn would grin when he read this letter. Evidence? Who had talked? She was sure Winborn would have her watched after Herman died. Nothing would give him more satisfaction than to see her without a nickel! After having free run of Herman's money, spending without thinking for the past years, such an income was a pittance! And this daughter of his to get a million!

A sound made her spin around.

Rolfe stood in the bedroom doorway, supporting himself on two heavy canes. In his white silk pyjamas with his skull-like head and his glaring eyes, he looked like a terrifying, revenging spirit.

'How dare you pry into my private papers!' he exclaimed harshly.

Fury, shame, fear and hatred exploded inside Helga as she jumped to her feet.

'And how dare you have me watched! Sully your name? Who cares a damn about your name? You are not even a man, you heartless computer! That's all you are . . . a money making computer! You haven't a shred of kindness nor understanding in you!'

Rolfe made an unsteady move forward, his eyes blazing.

'You whore!'

'I would rather be a whore than a crippled joke!' she screamed at him.

Then it happened.

Blood rushed to his face, his mouth twisted, the canes slipped out of his hands and clattered on the floor. He clutched at his chest. The agony that swept through his thin body made her close her eyes. Then he toppled forward, suddenly boneless and fell at her feet.

CHAPTER TWO

'WOULD he die?'

Helga looked at her gold and platinum, diamond studded watch Herman had given her: one of his many wedding presents. The time was 23.18.

Through the open window she could hear the murmur of voices. The arc lights for the television cameras made a pattern on the ceiling. The news had leaked: the jackal press had arrived, but the hotel manager had sealed off the top floor and all telephone calls were being screened.

'Would he die?'

This continual query hammered inside Helga's head.

Hinkle had been marvellously efficient. He had come within seconds, taken in the scene: Rolfe on the floor, she backed against the far wall. He had gone immediately to Rolfe, knelt, his fat fingers finding the pulse.

'Is he dead?' Helga had asked.

A brief shake of the head, then Hinkle had picked up the thin body as if it were weightless and had disappeared into the bedroom. She had braced herself, going to the telephone, she had asked the hall porter to send a doctor immediately to Mr. Rolfe's suite. The sharp intake of breath told her how startled the hall porter was. She had given him no time to ask questions. She had hung up.

Hinkle had appeared from the bedroom, unflustered, grave looking. She had told him she had called a doctor.

'May I suggest you return to your apartment, madame?' he said. 'Could you call Dr. Levi?'

'Is it a stroke?'

'I fear so, madame. Mr. Winborn and Mr. Loman should be informed.'

She had returned to her suite and had spoken to Dr. Levi.

Back in Paradise City, Dr. Levi had just finished dinner and had guests, but he had said he would charter an air taxi and would be with her in two hours. Winborn had been at the theatre and she had left a message for him to call her. Loman, his voice quivering with shock, had said he would take the executive jet and would arrive sometime early tomorrow. He had asked anxiously if the press knew. She had said not to her knowledge. 'This will shoot the market to hell,' he had moaned. Impatiently, she had hung up.

She had returned to Rolfe's suite. There had been a big coloured man wearing a peak cap, a gun on his hip, standing at the top of the stairs: another by the elevator. Both of them saluted her.

The manager of the hotel had been in the living-room. He had said that the doctor who had been called was with Mr. Rolfe. He had murmured sympathy, obviously worried. Helga paid no attention.

When Rolfe had surprised her, she had slammed the red folder shut. It was still on the desk like a red warning light. She had put it back in the drawer.

A heavily-built, youngish coloured man, sweating profusely, had come from the bedroom. He had introduced himself as Dr. Bellamy. She had seen he was in awe of her, nervous and worried. He had said her husband had suffered a massive stroke, everything that could be done would be done and he had hurried to the telephone.

She had gone to the bedroom door but Hinkle had appeared and had blocked her view.

'It would be better, madame, for you not to be here,' he said gently. 'Please rely on me.'

She had nodded.

'Dr. Levi is coming.' She had hesitated. 'Is he suffering?'

'No, madame.'

Listening, the manager had come to her.

'Let me take you back to your suite, Mrs. Rolfe.'

As she had moved across the room, Hinkle had closed the bedroom door. She had paused, then going to the desk, she had taken out the red folder and accompanied by the manager, she had returned to her suite.

At the door, the manager had said, 'I will see you are not disturbed. Mr. Rolfe's man will take all telephone calls. You have had no dinner. May I suggest . . .?'

'No, nothing and thank you.'

She had gone into her suite and had closed the door. It was then she had remembered her date with Harry Jackson and she felt a pang of frustrated disappointment. She had found there was a little vodka martini left in the shaker. She had drunk it, lit a cigarette and had sat down.

She had been sitting like that for the past two hours, nursing the red folder, smoking cigarette after cigarette.

Would he die?

Dr. Levi had arrived. He had seen her for only a few minutes. Her husband, he told her, had had a massive stroke. As soon as he considered it safe, he would be removed to the hospital. It was unfortunate the news had been leaked. Now that the press had arrived, it would be wise for her to remain in her apartment. The hotel management understood the situation. Security precautions would remain in operation. Would she like a tranquillizer? He would have news for her later that night.

At 21.00 when she should have been meeting Harry Jackson, the telephone bell had startled her. The operator, speaking in a hushed voice, asked her if she wanted to speak to Mr. Stanley Winborn.

Winborn had been alerted during the first act of the play. He had immediately returned home. She had told him what Dr. Levi had said.

'I have contacted Loman.' Wimborn's voice was cold. 'We will be with you as soon as possible.'

The gathering of the vultures, she thought.

The hotel manager had arrived carrying a plate of tiny sandwiches and a cocktail shaker on a tray.

'You need strength, Mrs. Rolfe,' he had said, putting down the tray. 'Please eat something,' and he had left.

She found she was ravenous and was irritated that the sandwiches were so small, but after drinking three vodka martinis and eating all the sandwiches, she was relaxed enough to open the red folder and to re-read Rolfe's letter to Winborn.

Would he die? she asked herself as she returned the letter to the folder. If he did her problems would be solved. Only Hinkle knew of the letter to Winborn. Hinkle? She thought about him. Could she rely on him to keep silent? Her mind went to Archer who had been the last person she imagined could or would turn to blackmail . . . yet he had. Hinkle? But it would be his word against hers and if she destroyed the letter surely that would be that. Winborn, of course, would believe Hinkle if Hinkle told him about the letter, but there would be nothing Winborn could do about it. He had Herman's original will. He would have to act on it. Sixty million dollars . . . but only if Herman died! Would he die? She beat her clenched fists together. What if he didn't die? He had seen the hatred in her eyes. The realization of her contempt and hatred of him had produced this stroke. She was sure of that. So if he recovered he would condemn her to the life of a nun. He could even make life so impossible she would have no alternative – as his daughter had had no alternative – but to leave him.

She looked around the big, luxurious room. She thought of many other similar rooms in similar hotels. She thought of the magnificent villa on its private island off Paradise City, the villa in Castagnola, the gracious penthouse in New York. She thought of the bows, the salutes, the smiles from head waiters, hall porters and even police: all attentive to her slightest whim. All that would go. She would have to begin life again and at forty-three, she shrank from the prospect. Not that she couldn't earn a good living. She had saved some money, she had something like three hundred thousand dollars worth of personal jewellery. Daunting though it was to contemplate returning to the life of cut-throat business, it wasn't that that made her flinch. It was the realization that she would no longer be pampered, fawned over Mrs. Herman Rolfe, the wife of one of the richest and most powerful men in the world.

But if he died!

She would have complete freedom and sixty million dollars! With her flair, her training in law and her drive she might even become as powerful as Rolfe. There were many opportunities when you had a capital of sixty million dollars!

If he died!

She looked at the red folder. Should she destroy the letter? Not yet, she told herself. If he recovered she would have to return the folder to his desk, but if he died, then she wouldn't hesitate to destroy it.

She looked around the room for a safe hiding place, then going to the closet, she took from it one of her suitcases which was now empty. She put the folder in the suitcase and put the suitcase under another empty suitcase. It would be safe there.

The time now was 23.40. How much longer would she have to wait? She began to pace up and down the big room, keeping away from the open window. She didn't want any of the waiting reporters to spot her. She was still pacing and thinking half an hour later when Dr. Levi tapped on the door.

'How is he?'

'It is too early yet to say,' Levi shut the door. 'I am sorry, Mrs. Rolfe but it is serious. It depends on what happens during the next two or three days. Everything is being done. If there is progress after tomorrow, there is hope. I will remain here. Dr. Bellamy is most competent. You must be patient, Mrs. Rolfe. You will be kept informed.'

'Two or three days?'

'It is possible that by tomorrow we will know.'

'I must be told!' she said. 'Serious? What does that mean?'

Dr. Levi took off his glasses and pinched the bridge of his nose. Without looking at her, he said, 'Complete paralysis of the right arm, certainly brain damage and possibly the loss of speech.' He then replaced his glasses, but still didn't look at her.

Helga felt a cold chill run through her. This was something she wouldn't wish on anyone, even Herman.

'But he has already almost lost the use of his legs,' she said, half to herself.

Dr. Levi said gently, 'It is a tragic thing, but I did warn him.'

'You mean he won't be able to speak again?'

'That remains to be seen. I fear not. I suggest you rest now, Mrs. Rolfe. There is nothing you can do. I have here something to make you sleep.'

'It would be kinder if he died,' she said and shivered. 'No legs, no speech, no right hand . . .'

Dr. Levi put a capsule on the table.

'Please take this, Mrs. Rolfe, and go to bed.'

When he had gone, she sat down, ignoring the capsule. As she sat there, her fists clenched in her lap, she willed him to die, not now for her sake, but for his.

Stanley Winborn told Helga that at the last moment it had been decided that Loman, as vice president of the Rolfe Electronic Corporation, would serve a more useful purpose by remaining in New York. Now that the news had leaked, the shares of the Corporation would come under pressure. That was inevitable, but it meant little: you had only to sneeze these days for the Dow Jones index to slide, but Loman should remain at the helm: Winborn used phrases like that.

He had arrived at the Diamond Beach hotel at 11.15. Looking through the slots of the sun blinds, keeping out of sight, Helga watched him get out of the Silver Shadow, pause to talk to the reporters who had been there now for the past fourteen hours.

Although she hated him, she had to admit that Stanley Winborn was a distinguished, handsome looking man with the touch of the elder statesman about him. He was tall and thin with thick dark hair with white wings, a cool aloof expression, always immaculately dressed and a razor sharp legal brain. He treated everyone, including Helga, with cold distant politeness. She couldn't remember ever seeing him smile, let alone laugh.

Having spent a few minutes with the reporters, allowing photographers to set off their flash lights, he disappeared into the hotel.

It was almost an hour before he came to her suite. No doubt, she thought, he had been consulting Dr. Levi. Winborn always obtained facts and information before he moved into action. While she waited, she glanced at the newspapers. The majority of them carried banner headlines:

HERMAN ROLFE: A STROKE

She thought of the avalanche of inquiries, condolences, telegrams, cables and letters this line of print would cause. She hoped they would be directed to the New York office and not here.

'A sorry affair,' Winborn said as he entered the suite and he murmured sympathy which irritated Helga. 'It appears to be serious.'

'Yes.'

'Is there anything I can do for you, Mrs. Rolfe?' The steel grey eyes ran over her. 'I am, of course at your disposal.'

'There is nothing, thank you.'

A pause, then Winborn said, 'Mr. Rolfe has just concluded an important contract with the Japanese government. He was about to send me the draft contract when this dreadful thing happened. The matter is urgent. Would you know where the draft is?'

Without thinking, Helga said, 'Hinkle will know.' As soon as she had said this, she realized the danger. If Winborn got talking to Hinkle about Herman's papers, there was a possibility that Hinkle might mention the damning letter, but she need not have worried.

Winborn lifted an eyebrow.

'I would prefer not to discuss Mr. Rolfe's affairs with a servant,' he said.

You goddamn snob! Helga thought, but thank God you are a snob!

'May I trouble you to come with me, Mrs. Rolfe,' Winborn went on, 'so that we can go through his papers? This draft needs my immediate attention.'

Another escape! If she hadn't had the foresight to remove the red folder, Winborn would have pounced on it.

'Yes, of course.'

They went into Rolfe's suite. The two uniformed guards were still at the head of the stairs and by the elevator. They saluted and Winborn who loved recognition, inclined his head. The door was opened by a fat, kindly-faced nurse who let them in.

'Please be as quiet as you can,' she said softly and returned to the bedroom, shutting the door.

Winborn stood by her side as Helga went through the contents of the drawers. The folder containing the Japanese contract was quickly found. Another folder lay beneath it with Swiss Portfolio printed on it.

'That reminds me,' Winborn said, his voice low. 'Loman tells me there is a two million loss on the Swiss account. Mr. Rolfe told him the loss was due to reckless speculation.'

She steadied her jumping nerves. At least Rolfe hadn't told the truth. Neither Loman nor Winborn knew of Archer's embezzlement.

She looked up.

'The Swiss portfolio is my affair, Mr. Winborn. I am aware what has been lost. I have already discussed this with my husband. This is my problem . . . not yours.'

A slight tightening of his lips, but nothing more. He inclined his head.

'Then I will leave you, Mrs. Rolfe.'

'Is there anything else?'

'Not immediately. Dr. Levi thinks that if there is any sign of improvement Mr. Rolfe should be moved back to Paradise City where he can receive even better attention than here. A decision may be made in a couple of days. I must fly back to Miami this evening. I can, of course, rely on you to keep me informed.'

'Yes.'

'Then you will excuse me? I have a number of telephone calls to make. I am in suite 14 should you want me.' He began to move to the door, then paused. 'As Mr. Rolfe's executor and legal adviser I think I should know if you are continuing to follow Mr. Archer's advice. Two million dollars is a heavy loss.'

She looked directly at him.

'You have no need as yet to act as an executor, Mr. Winborn, and I trust it will be many years to come before you have to,' she said quietly.

Again the tightening of the lips, then he said, 'I

28

hope so too, Mrs. Rolfe. Please excuse me,' and he left the room.

Helga relaxed back in the chair, drawing in a long, deep breath. She had acquitted herself well, she thought. If the letter had been found this dangerous man would have unsheathed his claws.

Returning to her suite, she found Hinkle waiting. He looked tired and his usual benign expression was less in evidence.

'How are you, madame?' he asked, coming forward.

'All right. And you, Hinkle?'

'It has been an anxious night, but now Mr. Rolfe appears less poorly, madame. We must not give up hope.'

'Did Dr. Levi tell you . . . paralysis?'

'Yes, madame. Quite shocking, but we mustn't dwell on it. May I suggest lunch on the terrace? The press people have gone. You won't be disturbed and the sun is good for you.'

'All right. Oddly enough, Hinkle, I feel hungry.'

'It is the strain, madame. It is understandable.'

Dear, kind Hinkle, she thought. If Herman died, she did hope Hinkle would stay with her.

'I suggest a little quail pâté, madame, then a steak *au poivre en chemise*. I will supervise the chef.' Hinkle's face darkened. 'He has little talent. Then a champagne sorbet. The wine here, I fear, is not to be trusted, but the Bollinger is acceptable.'

'It sounds wonderful, Hinkle.'

He turned to the table where a shaker and a glass stood on a silver tray. He poured a drink.

She studied his movements, looked searchingly at his fat, pink and white face. No, she thought, no blackmailer. No, this time I can be sure.

'You think of everything, Hinkle,' she said as he handed the glass to her.

'I like to think I do, madame.' A pause, then he went on, 'At the moment I am unable to help Mr. Rolfe. Regrettably he is out of my hands. I would be happy if you would call on my services, madame. It would give me considerable pleasure.'

'Thank you, Hinkle, I will.' Her quick active brain saw

her chance. She must get Hinkle firmly on her side. 'Mr. Winborn asked for some papers to do with a deal. I told him you were familiar with Mr. Rolfe's affairs but Mr. Winborn ...' She stopped, seeing a faint blush come to Hinkle's face. Looking away, she said, 'Mr. Winborn is a snob.'

She then looked at Hinkle and their eyes met.

'So I believe, madame,' he said, gave a little bow and moved to the door. 'Then lunch in half an hour.'

When he had gone, she went out on to the terrace and surveyed the beach, the crowds and the traffic.

'I think Hinkle is mine,' she said to herself.

After lunch, Dr. Levi came to see her. He told her the haemorrhage in the brain hadn't increased. This was an encouraging sign. He took off his glasses to pinch the bridge of his nose. But the hemiplegia was severe. However, in time some sort of recovery was possible.

'Two or three months could see a marked change,' he went on. 'I have asked Professor Bernstein to make himself available. He is the best man in Europe. The condition of Mr. Rolfe's heart, however, is not satisfactory so I don't want to raise hopes. All the same, under the intensive care treatment he is receiving, I am satisfied that he should be able to be moved within three days. Unfortunately I am unable to remain here any longer and I am anxious to get him to our hospital, but Dr. Bellamy is most competent and you can have complete confidence in him.'

Helga's mind worked swiftly.

'A marked change? What does that mean?'

'If his heart continues to withstand the shock he has had, I feel confident that he will regain his speech and the paralysis that has attacked his right side will be less severe.'

'Two or three months?'

'It could take longer but certainly not less.'

'You mean that for two or three months he will be unable to speak?'

'It is most unlikely: mumbling, of course, but nothing that could be understood. I mention this because Mr. Winborn is most anxious to consult him. I have warned Mr. Winborn not to attempt to persuade Mr. Rolfe to make any effort.'

Two or three months if his heart held out, Helga thought.

'Could I see him?' she asked, not wanting to but knowing it was the right thing to say.

'Unwise, Mrs. Rolfe. There is no need to distress yourself unnecessarily.' Dr. Levi replaced his glasses. 'You have no need to worry. Dr. Bellamy will be in constant touch with me. I will make a decision by Friday whether he can be moved or not.' He regarded her. 'Now, Mrs. Rolfe, you must not sit around in this room. You must get out and enjoy the beach and the sunshine.' He smiled. 'I don't want another important patient on my hands: one is quite enough. So attempt to enjoy yourself. Mr. Rolfe is not going to die.' He paused, realizing he was committing himself. 'Let me say he will certainly survive for a number of days and I have every hope he will live at least to the end of the year. What I am trying to say is you may leave the hotel, try to live normally knowing Mr. Rolfe is in expert hands.'

'You are most understanding and kind,' Helga said.

When he had gone, she went out on to the terrace, feeling the hot sun like a sensual caress.

If a heart attack doesn't kill him, she thought, then in two or three months time he would tell Winborn about his letter.

Well, a lot could happen in two or three months. She still had control of the Swiss portfolio: the stocks and bonds amounted to some fifteen million dollars. This was something she had to think about. She did her best thinking at night. So tonight, in bed, she would review her future. At the moment, it seemed to her she was holding trump cards: Herman unable to speak for say two months, the damning letter in her possession and the control of fifteen million dollars: all trump cards.

She went into her bedroom and changed into a bikini. She put on her beach wrap, then called the Hall porter.

'A beach buggy, please.'

'Certainly, Mrs. Rolfe: three minutes.'

If ever Herman regained his speech, this V.I.P. treatment would abruptly end. If she had asked for a sixty ton motor yacht there would have been no problem, but the magic key was trembling in balance.

31

When she left her suite she noticed the two security guards had gone. This gave her a feeling of relief. Until Herman died, he and she were no longer news.

She drove on to the beach, waving to the saluting policeman who had stopped the traffic for her, then she headed away from the crowd towards the deserted, distant dunes.

As she drove by the row of huts, she remembered Harry Jackson. Up to this moment he had gone completely out of her mind, but seeing the huts, remembering he had told her he had rented one of them, made her think of him with regret.

The morning's newspapers had carried photographs of her. By now Harry Jackson would know she was Mrs. Herman Rolfe. He was no longer safe to have an affair with. In spite of his frank, friendly face, she knew now she could take no risks and also there could now be no affairs in Nassau. She remembered she was being watched. She glanced over her shoulder. No one was following her. The empty beach stretched behind her, but that didn't mean someone with powerful field glasses wasn't keeping track of her. She felt a little spurt of fury. It was only in Europe that she really could be safe. Certainly not in Paradise City: that was the last place in which to misbehave.

She must find some excuse for a quick return to Switzerland as soon as she could. It would be difficult, but not impossible.

Leaving the beach buggy in the shade of a palm tree, she ran into the sea and swam vigorously, then turning on her back, she floated, letting the gentle swell rock her until, feeling the bite of the sun, she walked across the sand and sat down in the shade of the palm.

'Hi!' Harry Jackson, smiling, sun goggles in hand, wearing only swim trunks, came across the sand and joined her. 'Do you always stand up your dates?'

She looked up at him, her eyes taking in the tanned muscular body and fierce desire stabbed through her like the cruel thrust of a knife. She was glad she had put on her sun goggles for she was sure he would have seen the naked desire in her eyes.

'Hello,' she said. 'I'm sorry about last night.'

'I was kidding.' Jackson dropped down by her side, stretched out his long legs and rested himself on his elbows. 'I'm sorry about your husband, Mrs. Rolfe.'

Another escape, she thought. If I had gone out with this man last night we would have been lovers by now and that would have been very dangerous, he knowing who I am.

'You have been reading the newspapers?' she said, staring across the beach wondering if anyone was watching.

'Sure. I keep up-to-date.' He smiled at her. 'The most beautiful woman in the millionaire stakes: that's how they described you and I guess they're right.'

'There are other more beautiful women . . . Liz Taylor.'

'I haven't met her so I wouldn't know.' Jackson dug up a handful of dry sand and let it run through his fingers. 'How is your husband, Mrs. Rolfe? From the papers, he sounds real bad.'

She was certainly not going to discuss Herman's health with a kitchen equipment salesman.

'Are you enjoying your vacation, Mr. Jackson?' she asked. When the need arose she could put steel into her voice. She did so now.

'Excuse me, but I'm not just being curious. It's important to me to know.'

She looked swiftly at him. He was staring out to sea, relaxed, smiling: a good looking specimen of male flesh.

'Why should it be important to you?'

'A good question. You see, Mrs. Rolfe, I have a problem.'

Instinctively a red light began to flash in her mind.

'Should I be interested in your problems, Mr. Jackson?'

'Problem . . . not problems.' He dug more sand and allowed it to trickle between his fingers. 'I don't know. I'm wondering . . . you could be.'

'I don't think so. I have many problems of my own.' She abruptly stood up. 'Have a happy vacation. I must get back to my hotel.'

He looked up at her. The smile was a shade less friendly.

'Sure. I was just trying to decide whether to talk to you about my problem or to Mr. Stanley Winborn.'

She felt a little jolt that set her heart racing, but she was tough enough to keep her face expressionless. She reached for her wrap and put it on.

'Do you know Mr. Winborn?' she asked.

'I don't, and between you and me, Mrs. Rolfe, I'm not crazy to get to know him. He looks a pretty tough character. He doesn't look a helpful guy. Would you say that's right?' He smiled at her.

'I don't understand what you are talking about,' she said curtly. 'Well, I must be going.'

'Please yourself, Mrs. Rolfe. I can't stop you. I just thought you could be more helpful about my problem than Mr. Winborn, but if you're in a hurry, then I guess I'll have to take my chance with your attorney ... that's who he is, isn't he?'

Helga leaned against the fender of the beach buggy. She opened her bag, took out her gold cigarette case, took out a cigarette and lit it.

'Go ahead, Mr. Jackson: tell me about your problem.'

Jackson smiled up at her.

'You haven't only beauty, Mrs. Rolfe, you have brains: a very rare combination.'

She waited while he dug more sand.

'A couple of days ago, Mrs. Rolfe, your husband tele-phoned me and hired me to put you under surveillance,' Jackson said.

This time Helga couldn't quite conceal the shock. She dropped her cigarette, but she quickly recovered. With steady hands, aware Jackson was watching her admiringly, she found and lit another cigarette.

'Are you telling me you are the peeping Tom my husband hired?'

'Well, I'm called an inquiry agent,' Jackson said and chuckled. 'Peeping Tom is all right though: not a bad de-scription.'

'I was under the impression you were a kitchen equipment salesman,' Helga said contemptuously, 'a considerable cut above a spy.'

Jackson laughed.

'You have a point there. Actually I was a kitchen equipment salesman but it was rough going. Agency work pays a lot better.'

'Spying on people doesn't bother you?' Helga asked, flicking ash on the sand.

'No more than you cheating your husband, Mrs. Rolfe,' Jackson returned, smiling at her. 'It's a job, although cheating isn't.'

She decided she was wasting time. This man, with his deceptively friendly smile, had the skin of an alligator.

'What is your problem, Mr. Jackson?'

'Yeah ... my problem. When Mr. Rolfe telephoned me I was pretty shaken. I am associated with Lawson's the New York inquiry agency and they recommended Mr. Rolfe to call me. You know, Mrs. Rolfe, big names awe me. I don't know why it is, but they do. Maybe, I'm a hick ... could be the answer. Anyway, when Mr. Rolfe dropped this assignment into my lap I kind of flipped my lid. All I could say was "Yes, Mr. Rolfe ... sure, Mr. Rolfe ... you can rely on me, Mr. Rolfe." You know ... like a hick.' He shook his head frowning. 'Well, he so flustered me with his grand manner, his curt voice – looking at me, Mrs. Rolfe, do you believe I could get flustered? That was what Mr. Rolfe did ... he flustered me.' He began to dig more sand. 'Anyway, I accepted the assignment, but there was no talk about a retainer or a fee ... are you getting the drift now, Mrs. Rolfe? I decided that I hadn't a thing to worry about. All I had to do was to put a tail on you, and after a week, shoot in an account for daily expenses along with my report. I told myself when dealing with a man of Mr. Rolfe's stature you don't ask for spot cash.'

Helga said nothing. She dropped the stub of her cigarette in the sand, aware of fury rising in her.

'Well, now Mr. Rolfe is laid low,' Jackson continued. 'You see my problem? From what I read, he is to be carted off before long to Paradise City. Now I have a living to make. I have hired a couple of guys to watch you and they have to be paid.' He smiled at her. 'I run the office you understand. I don't do the leg work. Now these guys cost. I should have asked Mr. Rolfe for a retainer, but as I explained I was flustered. So there it is. I've got two guys to pay and Mr. Rolfe ill. See my problem?'

Still Helga said nothing. This time her silence seemed to irritate Jackson. He shifted restlessly and dug more sand more violently.

'I've been trying to make up my mind whether to ask you for the retainer or Mr. Winborn,' he said after a long pause.

Helga flicked more ash and waited.

'Am I getting to you, Mrs. Rolfe?' His voice hardened and the smile had gone.

'Let us say, Mr. Jackson, that I am listening,' Helga said quietly.

'Yeah ... beauty, brains and toughness. That's fine with me. Mrs. Rolfe. Let me lay it on the line: ten thousand dollars, I call off my watch dogs, you can have fun and when Mr. Rolfe is well again, I send him a negative report. Fair enough?'

Helga regarded him, her eyes glittering.

'I suggest you contact Mr. Winborn and ask him for your money. Mr. Winborn doesn't leave for New York until this evening so you will have time. And there is one thing you should know about me which you seemed to have missed. To me blackmail is a four letter word and a blackmailer is a four letter man.'

As she got into the beach buggy, Jackson laughed.

'Well, it was a try, wasn't it?' he said. 'No harm in trying.'

Without looking at him, Helga drove fast back to the hotel.

'There are a number of telegrams which I have sent to your suite, Mrs. Rolfe,' the Hall porter said as he handed Helga her key. 'Mr. Winborn has been inquiring. He wishes to see you before he leaves.'

'Tell him, please, that I have returned and I will see him in half an hour,' Helga said.

The elevator was waiting as she walked quickly across the lobby, aware the chatter of voices had hushed and people were looking at her from the corners of their eyes.

Unlocking the door to her suite, she entered, glanced at the two piles of telegrams and cables on the table, grimaced and went into her bedroom. The avalanche had begun.

She took a shower, put on a blue linen dress, arranged her hair, looked at herself thoughtfully in the mirror and her lips twisted into a hard little smile.

Moving out on to the terrace, she sat in the shade of a sun umbrella, crossing her long, beautiful legs, and forced herself to relax.

In the future she must be much more careful about picking up strange men, she thought. This Jackson business could have ended in a disaster. She lit a cigarette. She must control herself until she was once again in Europe.

Jackson!

He had certainly fooled her with his frank, friendly smile. Harmless! As harmless as a black mamba! She had handled him well, she thought, and was pleased with herself. *No harm trying.* The fool! He had nothing in writing from Herman: just a telephone call. It showed what a fool he was even to have thought he could get ten thousand dollars from her with such an empty threat. She was sure he wouldn't dare approach Winborn. Even he had said Winborn looked a hard character. Although Winborn, out of spite, might believe him, he would certainly give him no money. He would dismiss him with a flick of his fingers. The situation, at the time unpleasant, was now taken care of. Mr. Jackson could turn his attention to spying elsewhere. She was glad that he would be out of pocket.

But she really must control her feelings. This was the second time she had narrowly escaped being blackmailed. If only handsome, muscular men didn't react on her the way a drink reacted to an alcoholic: this was something she must fight, knowing she had told herself this over and over again.

At least she felt confident now that Jackson knew he wasn't going to get any money he would call off his spies, but she mustn't take any chances. She must return to Switzerland: there there were safe opportunities.

Winborn arrived at 17.45.

'The situation,' he began, once he had settled himself, 'is a little complicated. May I ask if you have a power of attorney on your husband's banking account?'

She shook her head.

'Nor have I nor Loman. This unexpected happening ties up Mr. Rolfe's personal account. There will be considerable expenses. How are you off for money, Mrs. Rolfe?'

'I have my own account but it is running low. I have access to the Swiss account. Dividends are continually coming in. I can transfer money from Switzerland to my account.'

Winborn lifted his eyebrows.

'With the regulations as they are, Mrs. Rolfe, I suggest that would be most unwise.'

She hadn't considered this and she was annoyed at her sloppy thinking.

'Yes, stupid of me.' She saw her opening. 'I could go to Lausanne and get traveller's cheques.'

He nodded.

'That would be the wisest thing to do. The Corporation will take care of Mr. Rolfe.' He looked at her. 'And you too, of course.'

'I prefer to have my own money,' Helga said curtly. 'When Herman is safely back home and out of danger, I will make a quick trip.'

Winborn turned a heavy gold signet ring on his little finger as he said, 'Dr. Levi appears to be more optimistic, but these next days will be anxious ones. Have you any idea how I can get in touch with his daughter, Sheila?'

Startled, Helga looked at him.

'None at all: I have never met her. Have you?'

'Yes, indeed: a remarkable young woman ... one might even say extraordinary.'

'Oh? In what way?' Helga was suddenly curious, knowing that this girl would inherit a million dollars.

Winborn continued to fidget with his ring.

'She took a first in History at Oxford. I understand she was the youngest ever to graduate. She took a brilliant degree in economics later. Both your husband and I expected her to do great things and there was an important position waiting for her in the corporation.' He lifted his shoulders in a resigned shrug. 'Unfortunately, she became involved in these tiresome anti-movements that seem to be

38

the disease of the young. Your husband always kept her well supplied with money and she used this money to further the cause of minority groups until she was finally arrested with others involved in gun smuggling. It cost a lot of money and trouble to keep her out of prison. Your husband and she quarrelled over this. He warned her that if she didn't conform to his plans for her he would cut her off. It was not the way to handle her. She walked out and I've heard nothing of her since.'

'Good for her,' Helga said and meant it.

'Yes . . . she has a lot of character, like her father. It does occur to me at this distressing time, Sheila who was and I hope still is fond of her father might want to see him and he her. That's why I am asking if you knew where she was.'

'I don't, but the news of his stroke must reach her. Every newspaper in the world will report it.'

'Yes. Well, we must wait and see.' He paused, then went on, 'I have a little puzzle you might help me to solve, Mrs. Rolfe. Nurse Fairely tells me that your husband is apparently trying to convey a message to her.'

Helga stiffened.

'Oh?'

'Nurse Fairely has considerable experience with patients suffering a stroke. She is used to their inarticulate sounds. She believes your husband is repeating continually the odd phrases: "Sin on. Better law", and she tells me he points to the bedroom door. These words convey nothing to me. Do they to you?'

Helga relaxed.

'Sin on. Better law?' She frowned. 'How odd. No, they mean nothing to me.'

'Well, perhaps Nurse Fairely will be able to enlighten us later.' Winborn glanced at his watch. 'I must go, Mrs. Rolfe.'

He spent a few more minutes assuring her the corporation was in excellent hands, that she had only to telephone him if she were in need of assistance and that Dr. Levi had promised to keep in touch with him. All this was said in a cold, polite voice while he stood, gazing down at her with his steely grey eyes.

When he had gone, Hinkle appeared with a shaker and a glass on a tray.

'I trust you had a pleasant swim, madame,' he said as he poured the drink.

'Yes, thank you, Hinkle.' She took the glass. 'Mr. Winborn has gone.'

A slight frown appeared on Hinkle's face, but it immediately disappeared.

'So I observed, madame.'

'He was asking if I knew where Sheila could be found. He thought she should be told. You wouldn't know by any chance?'

Hinkle inclined his head.

'Yes, I know, madame, Miss Sheila writes to me from time to time. She and I, I am happy to say, have never lost contact. Miss Sheila is good enough, so she tells me, to be fond of me.'

Helga smiled at him.

'That I can understand. Where is she?'

'In Paris, madame. Excuse me if I don't give you the address. She gave it to me in confidence.'

'Of course. Do you think she would want to see her father?'

'I trust so, madame. I have already written to her, explaining Mr. Rolfe's condition. It is for her to decide. I would like to think she will come, but there could be financial difficulties. Miss Sheila appears to be living rough.' Hinkle looked disapproving. 'That, I believe, is the phrase. She may not be able to raise the money for the fare.'

'I could send her the money.'

Hinkle shook his head.

'I feel that would be unwise. If I may suggest, madame, it is better to wait and see if she replies to my letter. If she does and needs money, may I approach you?'

'Of course.'

He nodded, his face showing relief and satisfaction.

'Will you be dining in, madame?'

She thought of the long lonely hours ahead of her, but why go out and risk male temptation? It would be much safer to eat a solitary meal on the terrace and then go to bed with a book.

'Yes. I feel like an early night.'

'Then I suggest something light: perhaps an omelette with truffles and a little lobster meat. I will cook it myself.'

'I'm dying to have one of your omelettes again, Hinkle.'

She couldn't have said anything nicer to him. When he had gone, she thought of Sheila who didn't know she was going to inherit a million dollars. Suddenly Helga frowned. The girl wouldn't get her money if Herman died speechless, unless his letter reached Winborn, and if it reached Winborn, she (Helga) would be condemned to the life of a nun. For some minutes, she considered this, then she decided that she herself could give the girl the money once she inherited the sixty million dollars . . . no problem.

Her mind switched to what Winborn had said. What could this odd message mean that Herman was trying to convey to the nurse?

'Sin on. Better law.'

She repeated it several times aloud, then she started to her feet.

Of course!

He was trying to say: *Winborn. Letter. Drawer.* He had pointed not to the bedroom door as the nurse had thought, but to the living room!

She must give the red folder to the manager to keep in the hotel safe. She should have done this before.

Putting down her drink, she went into her bedroom, opened the closet and took out the suitcase. She lifted the lid.

She stood motionless, staring into the empty suitcase, her heart racing.

The red folder had gone!

41

CHAPTER THREE

IT took Helga less than five minutes of feverish searching to convince herself that the folder containing Herman's letter to Winborn had been stolen.

Feeling cold, her fists clenched, her face a hard mask, she walked back into the living room and sat down.

Who could have stolen it?

Winborn? Unthinkable? Hinkle? Her eyes narrowed as she thought. He knew the contents of the letter. Had he discovered she had taken it and had decided to put it out of her reach should she be tempted to destroy it? She considered this, but she couldn't imagine Hinkle searching her bedroom before coming on the apparently empty suitcase. No ... she refused to believe Hinkle would do such a thing. Then who?

She then remembered the hotel manager had seen her take the folder from the desk and take it to her suite, but she couldn't believe the manager of a hotel of this standing ... no, that was ridiculous. Then she recalled the two security guards who had been guarding the corridor had been withdrawn. So while she had been swimming, anyone could have come to the top floor and entered her suite.

She lit a cigarette and forced away the teeth of panic that threatened to nibble. She had to face the fact that the letter had gone, that she had lost one of her trump cards. Now what was going to happen? Would the thief send the letter to Winborn? She was far too cynical to believe that. Once again the stage was set for blackmail. Her lips twisted into a hard, little smile.

The discreet buzz of the telephone made her stiffen. She hesitated, then lifted the receiver.

'Mr. Winborn is calling, Mrs. Rolfe,' the operator told her. 'Should I put him through?'

Winborn?

Helga frowned. Winborn should be winging his way back to Miami by now.

'Are you sure there isn't a mistake? Mr. Winborn has left for Miami.'

'The gentleman says he is Mr. Stanley Winborn, and it is urgent.'

'Put him on.'

There was a pause, then she heard the operator say, 'Go ahead, Mr. Winborn.'

Helga said, 'Hello?'

'Hi! Don't hang up. I've got something you want.' She recognized Harry Jackson's breezy voice.

Here it is, she thought and the steel in her hardened. She should have thought of him, the harmless black mamba.

'You don't waste much time, do you, Mr. Jackson?' she said, her voice steady while her eyes snapped fire.

He laughed his casual laugh.

'You can say that again, Mrs. Rolfe.'

She heard a tap on the door, then the door opened and Hinkle came in pushing the service trolley.

'I can't talk now,' she said curtly. 'Call me back in an hour,' and she hung up.

'The omelette should be eaten immediately, madame,' Hinkle said as he fussed with a chair. 'To allow it to cool will spoil it.'

She braced herself, got up and walked to the chair he had placed before the table. As she sat down, he spread the serviette across her lap.

'And you spoil me too,' she said. Was it her voice saying this?

'It is my pleasure, madame,' Hinkle said. He lifted the silver cover and with loving hands served the omelette. He poured wine, then stood back, his pudgy hands clasped in front of him.

It said a lot for Helga's iron control that she was able to eat the omelette and chat with Hinkle.

When she had finally forced down the last mouthful, she praised his cooking, refused coffee and thankfully wished him good night.

When he had gone, she went out on to the terrace. It was a hot night with a brilliant moon. People still bathed. Their excited, happy voices floated up to her, emphasising her loneliness.

I've got something for you.

It could only be Herman's letter to Winborn. How had he obtained it? There would be a blackmail demand ... that was for sure. What was she going to do? If he sent the letter to Winborn her life, as she knew it, would come to a grinding halt. The Swiss portfolio would be taken from her. The trip to Lausanne that she was now longing for would be off. She would have to ask Winborn to finance her until Herman recovered sufficiently to take over. Don't panic, she told herself. The letter hadn't yet reached Winborn. First, she must listen to Jackson's terms. Was an ex-salesman of kitchen equipment going to dictate the kind of life she would lead? Getting up, she moved around the big terrace, thinking. She now had to control herself and her active mind probed for a way out. Making a decision, she went into the living room and called the Head porter.

'Yes, Mrs. Rolfe?' The bow was in the voice.

'I want a pocket sized tape recorder with a microphone,' she said. 'The microphone must be very sensitive. I want it within an hour.'

There was a slight pause, then the gears slipped into mesh. 'It will be arranged immediately, Mrs. Rolfe.'

'Thank you,' and she hung up.

She went to her closet and selected a white linen handbag. With a pair of scissors, she cut away the lining. If the microphone was sensitive enough the recorder could record while out of sight in the bag.

For the moment, there was nothing else she could do. If Jackson sent the letter to Winborn, she could nail him as a blackmailer. She would have to be careful how she handled the transaction he would propose. She would have to direct the conversation so that he incriminated himself. She knew about voice prints. The police would be able to identify him as the blackmailer.

Forty minutes crawled by, then the assistant manager, a tall, willowy, blond man tapped on the door.

'I understand, Mrs. Rolfe, you require a tape recorder. I have a selection,' and he set four tiny recorders down on the table.

'Which is the most sensitive?' she asked.

'I believe this one.' He pointed to a recorder, slightly larger than the other three.

'Thank you . . . leave them.' She smiled at him. 'I will play with them.'

'You understand how they operate, Mrs. Rolfe?'

'I am familiar with recorders.'

When he had gone, she experimented with the recorders, putting each in turn in her handbag and talking. It was while she was testing the last recorder that the telephone bell buzzed.

'Mr. Winborn calling, Mrs. Rolfe.'

She glanced at her watch: exactly an hour.'

'I will speak to him.'

Jackson came on the line.

'Listen, baby, I don't like being told to wait.' His voice sounded hard. 'Is that understood?'

'I was under the impression, Mr. Jackson,' Helga said icily, 'that salesmen, no matter how inefficient, are trained, at least, to be courteous. You seem to have lost your manners – if you ever had any. You will not call me baby. Is that understood?'

A pause, then Jackson laughed.

'Beautiful, brainy and tough. Okay, Mrs. Rolfe, forget it. Do you feel like a swim tonight? The same place?'

Her mind worked swiftly. It would be too dangerous to meet him in that lonely spot. No, she would face him on ground of her own choosing.

'Come to my suite, Mr. Jackson. We can talk on the terrace.'

He laughed again.

'Not such a hot idea. I have your reputation to think of and mine too. How's about the Pearl in the Oyster restaurant? We could have coffee.'

'In half an hour,' Helga said and hung up.

She played back the recordings. The recorder the assistant manager had recommended gave a remarkably clear play back. She put it in her bag, added cigarettes, a lighter, her purse, her compact and a handkerchief, then slipping on a light wrap, she went down to the lobby.

She intended to be the first to arrive at the restaurant. The Cadillac taxi pulled up outside the Pearl in the Oyster, one of Nassau's popular night spots. The Maitre d'hotel immediately recognized her.

'Why, Mrs. Rolfe, this is a great pleasure,' he said, his black face lighting up.

'I am meeting a Mr. Jackson,' Helga said. 'We will only have coffee. Could you let me have a quiet table, please?'

'Of course, Mrs. Rolfe, if you wouldn't mind being upstairs. We have alcoves there.' The Maitre d'hotel's face went blank, telling Helga how startled he was.

He led the way up the stairs and to an alcove that overlooked the main dining room.

'Would this do?'

She paused to survey the crowd below, aware of the noise of voices, the clatter of plates and cutlery. This noise could wreck the recording.

'I would prefer somewhere quieter,' she said.

'Then may I suggest the after-casino balcony? No one is there at present, Mrs. Rolfe. Perhaps you would prefer that?'

'Let me see it.'

He took her along a corridor to a broad balcony overlooking the beach and sea. Apart from four or five coloured waiters, the place was deserted.

'This will do, and thank you.' She slid a ten dollar bill into his hand. 'Will you please bring Mr. Jackson to me when he arrives? Coffee and brandy.'

Jackson arrived ten minutes later. She had put her handbag on the table and as she saw him coming along the corridor, she quickly switched on the recorder. It would run for thirty minutes and that, she thought, would be long enough to incriminate him.

Jackson was wearing a freshly pressed white suit, a blue and white checkered shirt and a red tie. He looked handsome and presentable. At any other time, he would have set Helga's blood on fire.

'Hi, there,' he said, waving away the Maitre d'hotel.

'Have I kept you waiting?' The wide, friendly smile was in evidence as he sat down.

She looked beyond him at the Maitre d'hotel.

'We will have coffee now, please.'

'Certainly, Mrs. Rolfe.'

When he had gone, Helga looked directly at Jackson. He was completely relaxed, his big hands on the table, very confident. Her eyes swept over him. How deceptive men could be, she thought. Who would imagine this frame of muscle and flesh and good looks housed the mind of a blackmailer?

'How's Mr. Rolfe?' Jackson asked. 'Any improvement?'

'How is the peeping Tom agency, Mr. Jackson?' Helga asked politely. 'Better prospects?'

He gave her a sharp look, then laughed.

'I'll say . . .'

A waiter brought coffee and two brandies in balloon glasses.

They waited until he had gone, then Helga said, 'It is just possible you might imagine that this meeting is distasteful to me. Would you please tell me why you arranged it?'

'I was under the impression, Mrs. Rolfe, that you set it up,' Jackson said, smiling at her. 'You need not have come.'

A point to him, Helga thought. She mustn't waste time.

'You said you have something I wanted . . . what is it?' She dropped sugar into her coffee.

'A good question.' He sipped his coffee, crossed one long leg over the other and continued to smile at her. She longed to slap his handsome face. 'When you gave me the brush off this afternoon, Mrs. Rolfe, I was ready to call it quits. You were in an iron-clad position. I had nothing in writing from Mr. Rolfe. I wasn't going to tangle with Winborn. I steer clear of tough cookies. So I was all set to kiss my retainer good-bye.' He picked up his glass of brandy and sniffed at it. 'So you have the complete photo, Mrs. Rolfe, let me tell you how I operate. I don't have a regular staff. I have contacts. As an investigator it is a must to have a contact in every luxury hotel. I regard these contacts as invisible people . . . the staff. People who can go in and out of rooms, walk down corridors, clean the baths and still remain invisible to the guests. It costs me five hundred dollars, and that's money to me, Mrs. Rolfe, to buy the services of the fink who cleans your room, cleans your bath and makes your bed. Now this fink is a half-caste West Indian who wants nothing in life except a Harley-Davidson Electra Glide motorcycle. These bikes cost. He has been saving and saving, but he was well short of the target. Then this week a model arrived out here: just one, you understand, Mrs. Rolfe. He knew if he didn't grab it, he would have to wait maybe another six months. Well, you know how it is ... people, these days, can't wait, so I gave him the money and he bought the bike. In return, he did this favour. You know, you do something nice, the other guy repays you ... quid pro quo ... does that surprise you ... me talking like this ... quid pro quo? I've had some kind of education: not much more than quid pro quo, but some.' He sipped the brandy, then held up the glass to stare at it. 'Pretty good, but then that's how the cards fall for you, Mrs. Rolfe. You say brandy and you get the best. I say brandy and I get hogswash.'

Helga wanted a cigarette, but she couldn't touch her bag while the recorder was working. She controlled the urge and looked out at the deserted beach, at the moonlit sea and she listened.

'So this fink who cleans your room took a look around. The system is, Mrs. Rolfe, that as soon as a guest leaves the room, the fink moves in and puts it straight. He is an intelligent fink and he is anxious to please. I tell him: "Look around. If there is anything that looks important, I want it." So he stared at me with his intelligent black eyes and asks: "What's important?" I tell him: "I want to nail this baby. Love letters would do fine."' Jackson laughed. 'You know, Mrs. Rolfe, this was a shot at the moon. I hadn't any hope he would land a fish, but he did. When he gave me this letter from your husband to Winborn, I hit the roof.' He paused to sip more brandy. 'Am I reaching you, Mrs. Rolfe?'

So that was how it was done, Helga thought. Go on talking, snake, you're cutting your own throat.

'I'm listening,' she said.

'I bet you are.' Jackson laughed. 'So I have the letter.

Pretty strong stuff, isn't it? If this Winborn character gets it, seems to me you will be out in the cold.'

Thinking of the revolving tape, Helga hurried the conversation along.

'You could be right,' she said. 'This is blackmail, of course. How much, Mr. Jackson?'

'But didn't you tell me you never paid blackmail?' Jackson asked, his smile jeering.

'There are times when even the best generals lose a battle,' Helga said. 'How much?'

'You surprise me.' Jackson studied her thoughtfully. 'I thought you would try a wriggle.'

'I am not interested in your thinking,' Helga said, her voice steely. 'How much?'

The jeering smile slipped a little.

'Frankly, if it was only between you and me, Mrs. Rolfe, I would give you this letter for nothing. I would expect you to give me my retainer of ten thousand dollars ... my out of pocket expenses. That would be fair, wouldn't it?'

Helga said nothing. She sipped her brandy, longed for a cigarette, her face wooden.

'But this fink has ambitions,' Jackson went on. 'Can you imagine what he did? He took two photocopies of the letter, gave me one and here's one for you.' He took from his wallet a folded paper and pushed it across the table to Helga who took it, glanced at it and saw it was a copy of Herman's letter. 'Frankly, Mrs. Rolfe, I didn't imagine a half-caste fink would have had the brains to set up a thing like this. He is more ambitious than I am. As I've said, I'd be happy to get my retainer, but he has other ideas.'

Helga turned her cold look on him.

'So?'

'This fink tells me that the letter is a gold mine. Now when a half-caste boy talks about a gold mine, I don't pay a lot of attention, but when he started to elaborate, I took notice.' Jackson shook his head, finished his brandy and smiled at her. 'I guess he has bigger ideas than I have.'

This is almost too good to be true, Helga thought. As he sits there, shooting off his mouth, he is cutting his throat.

She could imagine the police descending on him. She imagined them picking up this hotel servant. To hell with Herman's money! To see this smart alec snake and his fink in court would repay even the loss of sixty million dollars ... stupid, angry thinking, but that was how she felt at this moment.

'He has?' she said quietly. 'How big? Couldn't you stop this yakking, Mr. Jackson, and tell me what it will cost to get this letter back?'

Just for a moment, Jackson looked uneasy, then the confident grin returned.

'Yeah ... I do run on. Well, for me, I want ten thousand dollars by tomorrow, not later than midday. I want it in cash. That will take care of my expenses which will be fine with me. Leave the money in an envelope with the Hall porter.' He looked at her. 'Okay?'

Helga inclined her head.

'Now the fink ... this is more tricky. As I've explained, Mrs. Rolfe, I hadn't an idea how his mind would work. Anyway, he has talked around and he's learned what a big shot you have married. He knows now that your husband is loaded. He won't part with the letter for less than five hundred thousand. Could anything be more crazy? I tried to talk sense into him, but he won't listen. I'm sorry, Mrs. Rolfe, but that's the way it is. If you want the letter, it'll cost you five hundred thousand, plus my ten thousand.'

Helga kept her face expressionless, but the shock was severe.

After a pause, she said, 'I find it hard to believe a coloured servant should think in such big terms.'

Jackson nodded.

'That makes two of us, Mrs. Rolfe. I was knocked for a loop, but that's how the cookie crumbles.'

'And this coloured boy gets all this money? Aren't you being very modest, Mr. Jackson?'

He laughed.

'Yeah: you could say that, but I only want my expenses. I like my job. I'm not ambitious. Frankly, I'm sorry I've got snarled up with this fink. Between us we could have settled this thing for ten thousand. If you had agreed last night instead of getting on your high horse, I wouldn't have told him to search your room.'

Helga regarded him.

'Aren't you talking too much, Mr. Jackson? You are letting your tongue run away. It was while we were talking on the beach that this fink, as you call him, was searching my room. That tells me you and he were working together and I am quite sure you and he will share whatever I pay.'

Again the confident smile slipped. He looked away from her, thought for a long moment, then the smile switched on again.

'As I've already said, Mrs. Rolfe, you have brains. Okay I'll put it on the line. It was the fink's idea. I wouldn't have thought of it, but when he said you would pay, I did think about it. With all this money coming to you when your husband kicks off, I saw the fink had an idea. He couldn't handle you. I saw that, so after thinking, I told him I would set up the deal and he and I would go fifty-fifty. So, Mrs. Rolfe, if you want the letter you give us ten thousand tomorrow and five hundred thousand in bearer bonds in ten days time.'

'And I get the letter?'

'Sure . . . no fooling. You get the letter.'

Helga drew in a deep breath.

She had him now! If she had to lose Herman's money, at least this snake would land in jail!

'All right. The money will be with the Hall porter by twelve o'clock tomorrow.' She got to her feet.

'So it's a deal?' Jackson asked her, smiling at her.

'It's a deal.'

As she reached for her handbag, he beat her to it. His big hand dropped on the bag as he continued to smile at her.

'No, Mrs. Rolfe. Not as easy as that,' he said. 'You are way out of my league. You caused a lot of uproar in the hotel when you asked for a sensitive recorder. The fink telephoned me.'

He took the recorder from her handbag, slipped out the tape, put the recorder back into her bag and the tape into his pocket.

Then he leaned forward, his handsome face a sudden snarling mask that chilled her.

'You are dealing with a professional, you stupid bitch!' he said softly. 'Don't ever try tricks with me. Ten thousand tomorrow or you'll be out in the cold.' As he got to his feet, he suddenly grinned, his friendly grin. 'Good night, baby, sleep alone,' and he left her, staring after him.

As Helga walked into the hotel lobby, the Hall porter came from behind his desk. Seeing he wanted to speak to her, she paused.

'There is an urgent call from Mr. Winborn, madame. He is staying the night at the Sonesta Beach hotel, Miami. He asks if you would please call him back.'

'Thank you.' She moved to the elevator. In her apartment she walked out on to the terrace. She sat down, half aware of the big floating moon, its reflection on the sea and the strident shouts of the night bathers.

Ten thousand dollars presented no problem ... but five hundred thousand!

Was she going to submit to blackmail?

She lit a cigarette. She never felt so alone. She thought bitterly that she had always been alone. The only child, her brilliance had cut her off from other children, her father had been interested only in his business; her mother only interested in the church. Always loneliness, plus this damnable sexual urge that had tormented her into dangerous adventures.

Face it, she said to herself, you are on your own: there is no one to help you: you are in a hell of a spot, so what are you going to do about it?

Thinking, she realized that even if Herman died this night, she would have Jackson and this half-caste on her back for life. They would give her the original letter but keep a photocopy. If she refused further demands and they sent Winborn the photocopy, he would take action. With his legal know-how and his spite, he would begin legal proceedings, especially if the hotel manager confirmed that she had taken the letter. Winborn could block her from the sixty million dollars!

She sat still, thinking, gathering her strength and her confidence in herself. This was going to be a lonely battle, she told herself. She had said to Jackson 'The best of generals lose battles.' But now she was determined this was the one battle she would not lose.

She returned to the living room and asked the telephone operator to connect her with the Sonesta Beach hotel.

'I want to speak to Mr. Stanley Winborn.'

There was a delay. Calm, she smoked and stared out at the moonlit sea. She told herself: 'I have so much to lose. I can afford to take risks. If I do lose, I'll make sure no one gains.'

When Winborn came on the line, she said, 'This is Mrs. Rolfe.'

'I'm sorry to trouble you, Mrs. Rolfe.' The cold voice came clearly over the line. She could imagine the steely grey eyes and the aloof, unfriendly expression. 'Could I ask you to do something for me?'

Surprised, she said, 'Of course.'

'While flying to Miami I got thinking about what your husband was trying to say. That odd phrase: "Sin on. Better law." After repeating it several times, it occurred to me he was trying to say, "Winborn. Letter. Drawer." '

You smart sonofabitch, Helga thought.

Forcing her voice to sound casual, she said, 'I would never have thought of that, Mr. Winborn.'

'I called Nurse Fairely. She asked Mr. Rolfe if that was what he was trying to say. By his reaction, it was. Nurse Fairely is sure that there is a letter for me in one of Mr. Rolfe's drawers.' A pause. 'May I ask you to check, Mrs. Rolfe?'

Not so smart, Helga thought. What you should do is to come back here and check yourself.

'We looked through all the drawers together, Mr. Winborn,' she said. 'There was no letter.'

'But there could be. We were looking for the Japanese contract.' A sharp note crept into Winborn's voice. 'Would you look more thoroughly?'

'Of course. If I find a letter for you, I will call you back.'

'I am sorry to bother you with this, but Nurse Fairely tells me Mr. Rolfe keeps on about this letter.'

'If I don't call back within an hour, you will know I haven't found it,' Helga said.

'Thank you, Mrs. Rolfe. How is he?'

'There is no change.'

She hung up and sat still for some moments. Winborn was no fool, but the immediate present was more important. She had sensed the suspicion in his voice. If he really became suspicious, he could make inquiries. The hotel manager, innocently, would tell him that she had taken the red folder from Mr. Rolfe's desk.

She hunched her shoulders. In spite of the hot, humid air, she felt cold. But this was no time to worry about Winborn. First, she had to deal with Jackson ... but how?

Suddenly, she felt exhausted. She remembered her father had often said to her, 'When you have a serious problem, don't make a quick decision ... always sleep on it.'

She got to her feet and walked into the bedroom.

'Sleep alone,' Jackson had said with a jeering grin.

If only there was a man here, she thought: a muscular, tall and virile man who would take her and send her on a sensational trip of relief, who would wash away the memory of Jackson's confident, jeering smile, her half-dead husband and this threat to her freedom.

She went into the bathroom, opened the mirror cabinet, took out a bottle of sleeping pills and shook two into her palm. She tossed the pills into her mouth and swallowed them. Stripping off her clothes, she took a shower, then went into the bedroom and dropped on to the bed.

The sounds of people enjoying themselves floated up through the open window. She could hear the roar of the passing traffic. Faintly, came the sound of the restaurant orchestra. It was playing 'I Follow My Secret Heart'.

Secret heart?

Yes, her heart was secret but also lonely.

She fought back tears. She despised self-pity. Impatient with herself, she reached out and turned off the light.

For some minutes, she lay in the dim light of the moon coming through the slots of the sun blinds, then the two pills mercifully took hold of her and she drifted off into an uneasy sleep.

It was when the effect of the pills was wearing off that she began to dream. She dreamed that she was in her father's office in Lausanne. He was sitting behind his big desk, tall, thin, upright, his face sternly handsome while she stood before him and told him about Jackson.

Although a brilliantly clever international lawyer, her father was given to old-fashioned clichés. In this dream he talked to her but his words didn't register. All she could hear were the clichés: 'What you put in, you take out.' 'What you lose on the swings, you gain on the roundabouts.' Then leaning forward, he said distinctly, 'Offence is better than defence.' She was waking as she heard his voice saying, 'Always know your enemy.'

She came awake with a start. The dream had been very real and she looked around the luxurious bedroom, not knowing where she was, then remembering. The sun was coming through the slots of the blinds. She looked at the clock on the bedside table: the time was 08.15

She lay still, thinking about her dream. *Know your enemy*. The drugged sleep had restored her energy. Her mind was clear. She lay thinking until 09.00, then she ordered coffee.

She was in the bathroom, finishing a quick toilet when she heard a tap on her door.

'Come in.'

She slipped on a wrap and came into the living room as Hinkle wheeled in a service trolley.

'Good morning, Hinkle,' she said. 'What is new?'

'Mr. Rolfe has passed a fair night,' Hinkle said as he poured the coffee. 'Dr. Bellamy will be seeing him this morning.'

She took the cup of coffee he handed to her.

'Could you find out two things for me, Hinkle?' she asked.

'Certainly, madame.'

'I want the name of the hotel detective and the name of the man who cleans this suite.'

Hinkle lifted his eyebrows: his way of expressing astonishment, but he said impassively, 'The hotel detective is Tom Henessey, madame. The cleaner is a young half-caste who they call Dick.'

'What a mine of information you are, Hinkle.'

He regarded her.

'Is there something wrong, madame?'

'Not at all. I believe in knowing the people who look after me.' She smiled at him.

'Yes, madame.' She could see she hadn't convinced him, but she was beyond caring. 'Will you be in for lunch?'

'No, I don't think I will. I'll either lunch in the grill-room or out.'

'Is there anything I can do for you, madame?'

How she longed to tell this solid, kindly man about Jackson. She shook her head.

'Give me one of your beautiful cocktails at six this evening,' she said. 'Nothing more. Do go out and enjoy yourself, Hinkle.'

'Thank you, madame. If there is nothing then I will take advantage of the sun.'

When he had gone, she finished her coffee, completed her toilet and then went along to Herman's suite.

Nurse Fairley, smiling, let her into the big living room.

'I've come to see if I can find this letter that is worrying my husband,' Helga said. 'How is he?'

'He is gaining strength, Mrs. Rolfe. He had a good night.'

'Can I see him?'

'I am sure he would be pleased to see you.'

Helga felt a little chill crawl up her spine. She braced herself as she crossed to the bedroom. Nurse Fairely tactfully went into the kitchenette.

Helga stood in the bedroom doorway, looking at her husband as he lay in the bed. She felt her heart contract. Could this ruin of a man be the mighty Herman Rolfe with all his millions, who with a flick of his fingers commanded attention, who held the magic key that unlocked the doors of the world? The skull-like face was now like a face modelled in wax and that had been exposed to a flame and had melted. The right side of the mouth was flaccid and hung open, showing his teeth and saliva dripped on to a towel on his white silk pyjamas. The useless right hand and arm lay on a pillow. The eyes that had always been cold, hard and forbidding were now like liquid pools of stagnant water, without life.

They stared at each other. Helga shivered, then pity for him rushed through her and she moved forward, but she stopped abruptly as his eyes lit up. His left hand moved and a bony finger pointed accusingly at her. The slack lips twisted and a sound came: *Bore!* which she knew meant whore.

'I am sorry, Herman,' she said, her voice husky. 'Really and truly, I am sorry. God help us both.'

His fingers flicked her away. The eyes expressed his dumb hatred. Shuddering, she stepped back and closed the door. For a long moment, she stood motionless, then controlling herself, she walked to the desk.

Nurse Fairely came from the kitchenette.

'It must be a shock to you, Mrs. Rolfe. So very sad ... such a fine man.'

'Yes.'

Helga made a show of looking through the papers in the drawers while the fat, amiable nurse stood watching her.

'There is no letter here. Please tell Mr. Rolfe.'

'Perhaps you would tell him, Mrs. Rolfe. It is odd. He is so insistent.'

'I can't face him again for the moment.' Helga's voice broke. 'You are at liberty to look through all these papers, nurse. Ask him if he would like you to do that.'

She was close to tears and turning away, she walked quickly back to her suite. It took her several minutes to recover, then with her capacity to absorb a shock, she switched her mind from her husband to Jackson. *Know your enemy.* That was to be her first move. Picking up the 'Room vacant: please service' card, she left the suite, hung the card on the door handle and rode down in the elevator to the lobby. She asked for a taxi and was driven to the Nassau National Bank. She told the taxi driver to wait. She entered the bank and arranged for fifteen thousand dollars to be available to her for the following day. As she left the bank, she saw across the road an automobile showroom. Above the door was a banner The Harley-Davidson Electra Glide motorcycle. Telling the taxi driver to wait, she crossed the road and entered the showroom. A young coloured salesman approached.

'I am interested in this motorcycle,' she said. 'May I see it?'

'The Electra Glide?' The salesman spread his hand in an exaggerated gesture of despair. 'We sold our only model, madame, but we will have another within a few months.'

'How disappointing. I wanted to see it,' Helga smiled. 'Perhaps the buyer would show it to me. Have you his name and address?'

'A moment, madame.' The salesman went away. He returned after a few minutes and handed her a card on which was written: Mr Richard Jones, 1150, North Beach Road, Nassau.

He then gave her an illustrated folder.

'You will find all the details here, madame. I would advise you to place an order with us without delay. There is considerable demand for this machine.'

Returning to the taxi, she told the driver to take her to North Beach road. It took ten minutes of driving out of the city before they reached the long, shabby street.

The driver, a West Indian, slowed and looked over his shoulder at her.

'You want some special number, missus?'

'Just drive along slowly,' she said.

Looking out of the window, she finally spotted No. 1150: a broken down bungalow with an iron corrugated roof, weeds in the garden, grey sheets hanging out to dry and a big, fat West Indian woman with grey in her hair, sitting on the stoop, reading a magazine.

Helga told the driver to take her back to the hotel. She had been absent half an hour. As she crossed to the elevator, the Hall porter materialized by her side.

'Excuse me, madame, but your room is being serviced. It won't be ready for you for another twenty minutes.'

'That's all right. I only want to pick up something. Thank you.' Giving him a smile, she entered the elevator and was whisked to the top floor.

There was a big service trolley outside her open door. Silently, she entered her suite. She heard movements in the bathroom. Shutting the door, she crossed to the desk on which lay the three recorders the assistant manager had left with her the previous evening. She switched one on, adjusted the volume control, then she walked silently into the bedroom. The bed had been stripped, a pile of towels lay outside the bathroom door. She could hear the sound of the spray swishing around in the bath.

She looked into the bathroom. A slim figure in white drill was bending over the bath, his head out of sight.

'Are you Jones?' she asked, pitching her voice high to get above the sound of the spray.

The figure started, dropped the spray, straightened and spun around.

She was confronted by a beautiful looking nineteen-year-old boy with thick black silky hair, big, fawn like eyes and perfectly moulded features.

They stared at each other.

A blackmailer? Helga thought. This she found hard to believe.

'Are you Jones?' she repeated.

The boy turned off the shower, licked his lips and nodded.

'All right, Jones, I want to talk to you.' She put steel in her voice. Turning, she walked into the sitting room.

There was a long pause while she stood with her back to the window, then he came out of the bedroom, his hands moving like agitated butterflies up and down his white jacket.

'Stand over there,' she said, pointing to the desk, then she sat down, opened her handbag and took out her cigarette case. He moved to the desk and stood staring at her. His olive skin glistened with sweat. She could see the rapid rise and fall of his tight jacket as he breathed.

'You own one of these?' She tossed the folder of the Harley-Davidson at his feet.

He stiffened and stared down at the coloured illustrations.

'Do you or don't you own one of these motorcycles?' she demanded, determined to give him no time to think.

In a small, low voice, he said, 'Yes, ma'm.'

'How did you pay for it?' The steel in her voice was like the lash of a whip.

His eyes widened and he took a step back.

'I – I saved for it, ma'm.'

'You saved for it?' She gave a scornful laugh. 'You ... living in a slum: your home with a tin roof. You saved more than four thousand dollars! I wonder what Mr. Henessey would say to that!'

His face turned grey.

'I saved for it, ma'm. I swear I did.'

'Listen to me, Jones,' she said. 'Yesterday morning, I left a valuable diamond ring in the bathroom. It is missing. Now I find that yesterday you paid for this motorcycle. I am accusing you of stealing my ring, selling it and with the money, you bought this motorcycle.'

He shut his eyes and swayed on his feet. For a moment she thought he was going to faint. Looking at him she felt desire stab at her. He was such a beautiful male. A half-caste. She wouldn't have known except for the silky black hair. She steeled herself.

'Isn't that what you did?'

'No, ma'am. I swear I didn't take your ring.'

'You seem good at swearing. All right, then let us see how Mr. Henessey deals with you. Let us see how the police will deal with you. I can't imagine anyone will believe you saved four thousand dollars.'

She got up and walked to the telephone.

'Ma'm ... please. I didn't take your ring.'

She paused by the telephone, her hand on the receiver, looking at him.

'But you did take something, didn't you?'

He seemed to shrivel in his white uniform as he nodded.

I'm half way there, she thought and released the telephone receiver.

'What did you take?'

In a whisper, he said, 'A red folder from your suitcase, ma'm.'

She returned to the chair and sat down.

'And what did you do with it?'

'I – I gave it to a man.'

'What man?'

He hesitated, then blurted out, 'Mr. Jackson.'

'Harry Jackson?'

'Yes, ma'am.'

'Why did you do that?'

Again he hesitated, then said, 'I wanted the bike. Mr. Jackson said he would give me the money if I would look around your suite for something important.'

'How much money was he going to give you?'

'Four thousand dollars, ma'm.'

'So you didn't save very much, did you ... less than two hundred dollars.'

'I – I don't earn much, ma'm.'

'Is it a fact, Jones, that Jackson employs you to spy on guests staying here?'

He licked his lips, looked imploringly at her, then said, 'This is the first time. I swear it's the first time.'

'Something important? Did he tell you what to look for?'

'He said love letters, ma'm or anything important.' He was now nearly crying. 'I know I shouldn't have done it, ma'm, but I did want the bike.'

'You read the contents of the folder?'

'I don't read handwriting so well. I saw it was about a will. It seemed important to me so I took it.'

She remembered Jackson's words: *He won't part with the letter for less than five hundred thousand. Could anything be more crazy? I tried to talk sense into him, but he won't listen.*

'Did you take a photocopy of the letter?'

He stared at her, his eyes bewildered.

'No, ma'm. I just gave Mr. Jackson the folder.'

'And he gave you four thousand dollars in cash?'

'Yes, ma'm.'

'Didn't you wonder why Jackson wanted something important from me? Didn't you wonder why he should give you so much money?'

'I wanted the bike.'

'Don't talk like a goddamn idiot!' Helga shouted at him. 'You must have wondered!'

He flinched.

'I – I thought he wanted to make trouble for you, ma'm. I had never seen you. I was just thinking of the bike.'

'Do you know what blackmail means?'

He flinched again.

'Yes, ma'm. It is a bad thing.'

'Didn't it occur to you that Jackson was planning to blackmail me?'

'He wouldn't do that, ma'm. Mr. Jackson is a nice fellow. He really is. He wouldn't do a thing like that.'

'And yet you did think he wanted to make trouble for me. What kind of trouble if it wasn't blackmail?'

He wrung his hands.

'I didn't think, ma'm. I just wanted the bike.'

'Jackson is now blackmailing me because of the letter you stole. He could go to jail for fourteen years . . . and so could you.'

Jones stared at her in horror.

'I just wanted the bike. I swear I didn't mean . . .'

'Oh, stop it! If you want to stay out of jail,' Helga said, getting to her feet, 'say nothing about this to anyone . . . especially Jackson. I will have another talk with you. In the meantime, get on with your work and wait until you hear from me. Do you understand?'

'Ma'm, I swear . . .'

'Do you understand?' The snap in her voice jolted him.

'Yes, ma'm.'

She picked up the tape recorder, switched it off and without looking at him, she left the suite.

CHAPTER FOUR

In the hotel lobby, Helga saw Dr. Bellamy coming from another elevator. The big, coloured doctor gave her an uneasy smile, changed direction and came over to her.

'I was inquiring for you, Mrs. Rolfe. I was told you were out.'

She looked up at him: here was a massive, well-built man, she thought, but not for her. He had no confidence in himself, and she could imagine he would sweat distressingly when making love.

'I've just returned. How is he, doctor?'

'His progress is reassuring. I am going to call Dr. Levi.' Bellamy moved with her away from the crowd to a quiet corner of the lounge. 'Please sit down, Mrs. Rolfe.'

She sat on a settee and opened her handbag for a cigarette. Dr. Bellamy joined her. He fumbled rather frantically for a match but she had already lighted her cigarette before he found one.

'I am suggesting to Dr. Levi that your husband could be moved from here to Paradise City hospital tomorrow. He has gained strength and under sedation, I feel sure the journey wouldn't distress him. However, there is a slight risk and this I will discuss with Dr. Levi. His heart . . .' Bellamy lifted his hands. 'And he is worrying. Nurse Fairely tells me he is worrying about a letter.'

'Yes.' Helga looked down at her hands. 'He has so many papers. I don't know which particular letter it is that is worrying him.'

A pause, then Dr. Bellamy said, 'If Dr. Levi agrees, you may make arrangements to leave sometime tomorrow.' He got to his feet. 'I will be in again this afternoon when I can tell you the exact arrangements.'

When he had gone, she walked out into the bright

sunshine and wandered in the hotel grounds. Already people were playing tennis and the swimming pool was crowded. She found a secluded seat under the shade of a palm, then making sure no one was near, she took out the tape recorder and played back the tape. The boy's frightened voice came to her clearly. It was an excellent recording and she nodded her satisfaction.

She thought of the boy. He couldn't be more than nineteen years of age. She was twenty-four years his senior: old enough to be his mother. The tormenting desires moved through her. None of her lovers had been so young as he and yet, sitting there in the shade, feeling the heat of the sun, she wanted him desperately. She could teach him how to make love, she thought. His confession on tape gave her complete control over him. He was a young animal and young animals could be trained. Tomorrow she would be back in the big villa in Paradise City. Herman would be in hospital. She sat still, thinking, then she finally gave a little nod. She would take the boy back to Paradise City. He was in no position to refuse. Once there ... she drew in a quick sharp breath. And besides, she would get him away from Jackson. That was important. Then she thought of the big, fat woman who must be the boy's mother. First, she must talk to her before telling the boy. Mothers could be difficult and suspicious. A West Indian! She was confident she could handle her. One thing at the time, she told herself. *Offence is better than defence*. She must stall Jackson and gain a little time.

Returning to her suite, she sat at the desk and turning on another of the recorders, still lying on the desk, she made a copy of the tape on the other recorder. She played the copy back, then satisfied, she put the original recorder in a stout envelope, sealed it, wrote her name on it, then put the second recorder in her bag. She picked up the telephone book. She found Jackson's telephone number and asked the operator to connect her.

Jackson's hearty voice came on the line.

'Discreet Inquiry Agency. Jackson talking. Good morning.'

'Good morning, Mr. Jackson, you sound full of life,' she said, steel in her voice.

'Who is that?' His voice sharpened.

'Don't you recognize my voice, Mr. Jackson? I thought you were a professional.'

'Oh . . . you.'

'Yes. Our little transaction will be slightly delayed. The bank here needs confirmation from my bank. Absurd, isn't it? I will call you again,' and she hung up.

That would take care of Jackson for a while. She was confident he wouldn't take action until he was sure she wasn't going to pay. The delay would give her a breathing space.

The telephone bell rang. She smiled. No, Mr. Jackson, you must learn to wait, she thought. Picking up the envelope, leaving the bell ringing, she went down to the lobby. The assistant manager was behind the reception desk.

'Please put this in your safe.' She handed him the envelope. 'I will be keeping all four recorders. They will make amusing presents. Please bill me.'

'Certainly, Mrs. Rolfe.'

He gave her a receipt which she put in her bag, then crossing to the Hall porter, she said, 'I want a small car, please. U-drive.'

'Certainly, madame. The new Buick perhaps?'

'No . . . a Mini will do.'

He lifted his eyebrows and bowed.

'In ten minutes, madame.'

'Would you know where Hinkle is?'

'On the second terrace, madame. Should I have him called?'

'No, thank you.'

She walked along the wide terrace, down the marble steps to the second terrace. She saw Hinkle sitting in a canvas chair, reading a book. He was wearing a white suit, a floppy bow tie and a large panama hat that rested on the back of his head. He looked like a bishop enjoying a well deserved vacation.

'What are you reading, Hinkle?' she asked.

He glanced up, then rose to his feet, removing his hat.

'An essay by John Locke, madame.'

'John Locke?'

65

'Yes, madame. A seventeenth-century English philosopher. In this essay he makes a case against the dogma of innate ideas and successfully proves that experience is the key of knowledge. It is remarkably interesting.'

Helga blinked.

'Why, Hinkle, I had no idea you were so learned.'

'I endeavour to improve my mind, madame. Was there something I can do for you?'

'Please sit down.' She sat in a chair near his. After hesitating, Hinkle lowered his portly frame into his chair, resting his hat on his knees. 'Dr. Bellamy tells me that Mr. Rolfe could be moved tomorrow to the Paradise City hospital providing Dr. Levi approves.'

Hinkle's face brightened.

'That is indeed good news.'

'Yes. It is very possible that you will have to attend Mr. Rolfe at the hospital. I want to engage extra staff to take over some of your less exacting duties at home, Hinkle.'

'Indeed, madame?' His voice turned chilly. 'I assure you I can manage perfectly well without additional staff.'

She expected opposition and was prepared to over-ride him. She was determined to have her way.

'There is a young boy working at the hotel,' she said curtly. 'He appears intelligent and a deserving case. When I can assist young people I like to do so. I am engaging him and I would like you to give him minor duties, Hinkle. Will you do that for me, please?'

Hinkle regarded her, saw the steel in her eyes, pursed his lips, then inclined his head.

'If that is your wish, madame.'

'No news of Miss Sheila?' She got to her feet.

'No, madame, not yet.' He too stood up.

'Then I will leave you with Mr. Locke.' She smiled. 'Dick Jones ... that's the boy's name. Pay him a hundred and all found and see he earns it, Hinkle. I will tell him to contact you.'

'Very well, madame.'

She returned to the hotel where she found a Mini-minor waiting. She thanked the Hall porter, then getting into the little car, she drove out of the city and to North Beach road.

66

Pulling up outside No. 1150, she got out of the car, opened the rickety gate and walked up the weedy path. She was aware that, opposite, coloured people, sitting on their stoops and on broken down verandas were gaping at her.

Paying no attention, she rapped on the front door. There was a pause, then the big, fat woman stood before her. Her eyes, black and a little bloodshot, widened at the sight of this slim, elegantly dressed white woman standing on her stoop.

'Mrs. Jones?' Helga smiled. 'I want to talk to you about Dick.'

The big woman regarded her. Since Helga last had seen her sitting on the stoop reading a magazine, she had changed into a red cotton dress, neat and clean and had wound a red and yellow handkerchief around her head.

'My son?' The voice was soft and rich. Helga could imagine a splendid contralto singing voice coming from this vast frame.

'I am Mrs. Herman Rolfe,' Helga said. 'Could we talk?'

'Mrs. Rolfe?' The eyes opened wide, then they shifted past Helga to the gaping people from the opposite houses. 'Come in, please.'

She led the way into a small, immaculately kept living room. There was a worn settee, two equally worn armchairs, an old T.V. set, a table on which stood a potted fern. On the wall was a large photograph of a tall, gay looking white man who smiled at Helga from the gilt frame. He wore shabby whites and there was an air of seediness in his jocular pose: a gay failure, Helga thought, probably a sugar planter who hadn't worked hard enough. Looking more closely at the photograph she saw from whom Dick Jones had got his good looks.

Mrs. Jones closed the door.

'I was reading about Mr. Rolfe this morning,' she said uneasily. 'Accept my condolences. It is a terrible thing for so fine a man to be stricken.'

'Thank you.'

There was a pause while the two women from utterly different worlds looked at each other, then Mrs. Jones said, 'Will you sit down, ma'm? This ain't much of a place but it is a home.'

'Is that your husband?' Helga asked as she sat down.

'That is Henry Jones . . . a no good man, but he gave me Dick, thank the Lord.'

'I want to talk to you about your son, Mrs. Jones,' Helga said. She felt in need of a cigarette, but had an instinctive feeling that this big, coloured woman wouldn't approve and she was anxious to have her approval. 'He does my suite at the hotel. He appears to me to be nicely mannered, intelligent and willing. I have a staff vacancy in my home in Paradise City . . . it is quite close to Miami. It would be a good opportunity for him, but before I talked to him, I felt I should first ask you.' Again she smiled. 'My major-domo would train your son, the pay would be good and there would be opportunities to travel to New York and Europe.'

'The good Lord bless me!' Mrs. Jones threw up her hands. 'Why should a grand lady like you, ma'am, be bothered with my son?'

Helga forced a laugh.

'I am like that, Mrs. Jones. With my money, I am able to help people. Watching your son work, I thought I could help him and he could help in my house. I know how mothers feel about their sons. I wouldn't want to be parted from a good son, but I would tell myself he should have his chance.'

Mrs. Jones looked directly at Helga, her eyes suddenly curious.

'You got kids, ma'm?'

You're over-talking, Helga told herself. Be careful.

'Unhappily no, but I do know how my father felt about me,' she said glibly.

'Dick is a good boy, ma'm,' Mrs. Jones said. 'He is an ambitious boy. Let me tell you something. He wanted a motorbike. He was crazy in the head to have this bike and he saved and he saved and he saved. They pay him seventy bucks at the hotel. That's good money for folk like us. He gives me thirty for his keep and he saves the rest. Then suddenly he comes home on this bike. He has saved a thousand bucks. Imagine that, ma'm! A thousand bucks! And do you know how he did it? No girls, no movies, no drinks, no cigarettes: scraping and saving and finally he has his bike. That's my son, ma'am, and a good son: couldn't be better.'

Looking at the proud, beaming face, Helga wondered how this believing mother would react if she knew her son's motorcycle had cost over four thousand dollars.

'I will pay him a hundred dollars and all found,' Helga said. 'He will, of course, have to work for it, but it will give him an opportunity to save.' She smiled. 'I would like to know if you have any objections to his working for me, Mrs. Jones.'

'Me?' The big woman shook her head. 'Ma'm, I come from Haiti. I worked on a sugar plantation. That's where I met Henry Jones. When my boy got to twelve years of age, I told myself I had to get out. I've saved and I came here. It was hard, but I wanted Dick to have a chance and he got this chance at the hotel. I live for my son, ma'm. You take him. I'll miss him, but to be able to go to New York, to Europe, to work for such fine people as the Rolfes ... this is something I couldn't even dream about.'

Helga got to her feet.

'Then I will arrange it. It is possible my husband and I will return to Paradise City tomorrow. Dick will come with us.'

Mrs. Jones put her big, work worn hands against her floppy bosom.

'So soon, ma'm?'

'Yes, but don't worry. He'll be all right.' Helga saw tears in the big, black eyes. 'You are an understanding and wonderful mother.'

Mrs. Jones drew herself up.

'I've got a wonderful son, ma'm. Nothing is too good for him, and thank you, ma'm and may the good Lord bless you.'

Returning to her hotel suite, Helga called the Housekeeper.

'I want to speak to the man who cleans my suite,' she said. 'Dick, I believe his name is. Please send him to me.'

'Is there something wrong, madame?' the housekeeper asked, alarm in her voice.

'Nothing is wrong. I wish to speak to him,' Helga said coldly.

'Certainly, madame. I will bring him to you immediately.'

'Send him to me. Your presence is not required,' and Helga hung up.

That will give them something to gossip about, she thought wryly, but she was beyond caring. She lit a cigarette and glanced at her watch. The time was 12.45. She felt in need of a drink, but decided to wait until she went down to the grill-room.

She waited three long minutes, then a soft tap came on the door.

'Come in,' she snapped.

Dick Jones entered slowly. His large dark eyes showed fear. In the hard sunlight flooding the big room his smooth skin sparkled with sweat.

'You wanted me, ma'm?' He could scarcely get the words out.

'Come in and shut the door.'

He moved further into the room, shut the door, then faced her.

'Now, listen to me, Jones. You are in trouble. I have been talking to your mother.' She saw him flinch. 'She believes you saved for your motorcycle. She believes what you told her: that it cost a thousand dollars. I know it cost more than four thousand dollars. I can prove this to her. What do you imagine she will say to you when she knows?'

He raised his hands imploringly.

'You wouldn't tell her, ma'm,' he said huskily. 'Please don't tell her.'

She took the recorder from her bag and set it on the table.

'Listen to this,' she said and switched on the play-back.

They remained still as their voices from the tape came distinctly to them both. When the tape finished, she switched off and looked at him.

'That is a confession, Jones, that you stole a valuable document.' She paused, then went on, 'The police would act on it. You and your friend Jackson could go to jail for at least fourteen years.'

He shivered.

'I just wanted the bike, ma'am.'

'To get your bike, you became a thief. Your mother told

me you are a wonderful son. Would she call a thief a wonderful son?'

He didn't say anything. He just stood there, sweating, his face ashen.

She let him sweat, then after a long pause, she said, 'You are going to leave here, Jones. You are going to work in my house in Paradise City. I want you away from Jackson. You will be paid, but you will do exactly as you're told. My major-domo, Mr. Hinkle, will take charge of you. I don't expect any trouble from you. Your mother has agreed that you should go. You will pack and be ready to leave tomorrow. Do you understand?'

His big black eyes widened.

'But, ma'm, I don't want to leave here. I have my home here. I have a good job here. I don't want to leave!'

'You should have thought of that before you turned thief,' Helga said ruthlessly. 'You will do what I say or I will turn you over to Mr. Henessey who will have no mercy on you, understand?'

He wrung his hands.

'What's to happen to my bike?' he said. 'Ma'm . . .'

'Damn your bloody bike!' Helga said furiously. 'Get out! You leave tomorrow!'

Staring at her, horrified, the boy backed to the door.

'Hinkle will send for you. Do exactly what he tells you and keep away from Jackson. Do you understand?'

'Yes, ma'm.'

'Then get out!'

Like a whipped puppy, he slunk out of the room.

She crushed out her cigarette, aware her hand was shaking. *Offence is better than defence.* She hated herself for terrifying this half-caste boy, but she had to do it. She was fighting for her future.

Consulting the telephone book she found the only other inquiry agency was The British Agency: Mr. Frank Gritten.

She asked the hotel operator to call the number. A woman answered: her voice brisk and efficient. 'British Agency. Can I help you?'

Helga hesitated, then she said, 'This is Mrs. Herman

Rolfe. I would like to consult Mr. Gritten this afternoon at three o'clock.'

'Mrs. Herman Rolfe?'

Helga could imagine the startled expression on the woman's face.

'Yes.'

'Certainly, Mrs. Rolfe. Mr. Gritten will be happy to see you at three o'clock.'

Helga hung up.

For a long moment, she sat motionless, thinking. She was taking a big risk, but she had everything to gain ... also everything to lose.

She left the suite and rode down to the lobby. She told the Hall porter she would have lunch in the grill-room and would he reserve a quiet table for her, then she went out on to the terrace. There was no sign of Hinkle. She couldn't imagine him in the sea, but nothing Hinkle might do would surprise her.

Driving the Mini, she went to the Nassau Bank and asked to speak to the manager. She was immediately shown into his office. The plaque on his desk told her his name was David Freeman: a stout, red-faced breezy Englishman who rose to his feet.

'Happy to see you here, Mrs. Rolfe,' he said offering her a chair. 'What may I do for you?'

As Helga sat down, she said, 'Yesterday I arranged to be able to cash fifteen thousand dollars with you, Mr. Freeman.'

'That is quite right. It has now been arranged.'

'I want ten thousand dollars in one thousand dollars bills. I want you to make a note of the numbers. I will sign the receipt and I want the numbers of the bills on the receipt.'

Freeman looked sharply at her, but seeing her cold, hard expression decided not to be curious.

'Certainly, Mrs. Rolfe. I will arrange this immediately.' He picked up the telephone receiver, issued instructions, then went on, 'I trust Mr. Rolfe is improving.'

'He is better, thank you.' Helga braced herself, 'Mr. Freeman, can you tell me the standing of The British Agency: the inquiry agents? Are they reliable?'

'Yes, Mrs. Rolfe.' Freeman's red face showed his surprise.

'You can have every confidence in them. Mr. Gritten, who runs the agency is an ex-Chief Inspector of the Nassau police. He happens to be an old friend of mine. He is utterly reliable, honest and a man of integrity.'

'There is also the Discreet Agency,' Helga said.

Freeman frowned.

'In confidence, that agency should be avoided.'

'Thank you.'

A girl came in with ten one-thousand dollar bills and the receipt which Helga signed, making sure the numbers of the bills were on the receipt. She put the bills in her bag.

Looking at Freeman with her cold, hard eyes, she said, 'Please keep this receipt safely, Mr. Freeman. It could figure in a criminal charge.'

'I understand, Mrs. Rolfe.' Freeman's bewildered expression clearly showed he wished he did understand, but this was Herman Rolfe's wife and you didn't ask questions when dealing with the wife of one of the richest men in the world.

Satisfied with her morning's activities, Helga returned to the hotel. She had a lonely vodka martini on the terrace, then a light lunch in the grill room. She had an hour before she called on the British Agency. She went to her suite and lying on the bed, rehearsed what she would say to Mr. Gritten.

The telephone buzzed, interrupting her thoughts.

'This is Dr. Bellamy, Mrs. Rolfe. I have consulted with Dr. Levi. He agrees that Mr. Rolfe can be moved. Dr. Levi has spoken to Mr. Winborn. There will be a chartered plane ready to leave tomorrow at 14.00.'

'This is splendid news, doctor, and thank you for all you have done.'

She called the Hall porter and asked him to find Hinkle. Ten minutes later Hinkle appeared. She told him what Dr. Bellamy had said.

'Please arrange for someone to pack my things tomorrow morning, Hinkle. Will you also interview this boy, Dick Jones and see he is ready to travel with us?'

Hinkle inclined his head.

'Yes, madame.'

73

When he had gone, she left the hotel and drove to Ocean avenue where the British Agency had their offices.

Checking the directory board she saw that the Discreet Inquiry agency: Mr. Harry Jackson was on the fourth floor. The British Agency: Mr. Frank Gritten was on the fifth floor.

She took the elevator to the fifth floor. An elderly, brisk woman welcomed her.

'Mr. Gritten is waiting for you, Mrs. Rolfe,' she said and led Helga into a large, sunny inner office.

The V.I.P. treatment, Helga thought. How long will it last?

Frank Gritten looked what he was: an ex-police officer, big, bulky, thick white hair, steady blue eyes and a calm expression that gave confidence.

'Please sit down, Mrs. Rolfe. I was sorry to read about Mr. Rolfe.'

Helga sat down. She looked directly at Gritten.

'I have been talking to Mr. Freeman of the Nassau Bank. He tells me I can have every confidence in you, Mr. Gritten.'

Gritten smiled.

'Freeman and I have been good friends for years.' He sat down at his desk. 'Yes, Mrs. Rolfe, you can have confidence in me. What can I do for you?'

'My husband, Mr. Gritten, has been ill for some time. This illness has affected his mind. He has got it into his head that I am being unfaithful to him,' Helga said and looked directly at the thoughtful, but probing policeman's eyes. 'Three days ago, he hired an inquiry agent to have me watched: a man called Harry Jackson.'

Gritten nodded, his face expressionless.

'A day after Mr. Rolfe hired this agent, he suffered this stroke. The agent is worried about his fees. According to him, no terms were discussed when my husband hired him. The agent has approached me, asking me to pay him. According to him he has worked for two days, hiring two people to watch me. I would like to ask you what would be a reasonable fee to pay him?'

Gritten reached for a battered pipe.

'May I have your permission to smoke, Mrs. Rolfe?'

74

She made an impatient movement.

'Of course.'

As he filled his pipe, he said, 'He is entitled to a retainer. The minimum would be three hundred dollars. For a client of Mr. Rolfe's standing, he could reasonably ask one thousand dollars. Then he would also be entitled to one hundred dollars a day expenses. For two days work, you can pay him one thousand, two hundred dollars, but not a dollar more.'

'Mr. Jackson is asking ten thousand dollars.'

Gritten's blue eyes turned steely.

'Have you proof of that, Mrs. Rolfe?'

'Nothing in writing.'

'You are speaking to me in confidence,' Gritten said, 'Nothing you say to me will leave this office. In my turn, I will speak to you in confidence. For the past six months, the Nassau police have been trying to revoke Jackson's licence. They suspect he is a blackmailer, but so far they have no proof. If you could and would supply evidence that he is asking for ten thousand dollars for two days' work, the police would put him out of business.'

'How is it then, Mr. Gritten, that he is associated with Lawson's Inquiry Agency in New York who I understand is a highly reputable firm?'

Gritten puffed at his pipe.

'Jackson was one of their operators. Four years ago he came down here and set up on his own. Lawson's backed him. A year ago, Jackson got himself involved with a night-club singer. She is demanding and to hold on to her, Jackson has been spending. He is now short of money and from what you are telling me, he appears no longer fussy how he gets it.'

Know your enemy! Helga felt a moment of triumph. The cards were falling her way.

'Do you know anything about this woman, Mr. Gritten?'

He removed his pipe and began to rub the bowl.

'If you want to put Jackson where he belongs, Mrs. Rolfe, you should come with me to the police who will give you every assistance and in the strictest confidence.'

'Thank you, Mr. Gritten, but I prefer to handle Jackson myself,' Helga said curtly. 'I would appreciate any information you can give me. Who is this woman?'

'Her name is Maria Lopez. She works at the Blue Bird club. She is married to Ed Lopez who owns and captains a mail boat that runs between here and the Out islands,' Gritten puffed at his pipe. 'Lopez is an interesting character. For sometime now, the police have been watching him. He leads a waterfront gang known as the Death's Heads. This gang terrorizes those who work on the waterfront, exacting dues, fines and so on. Lopez is as dangerous as a mad dog, Mrs. Rolfe.'

'Doesn't he care for his wife?'

Gritten smiled.

'Yes, he cares very much. As I said, Lopez is an interesting character. When he trusts someone, he trusts them. He trusts his wife.'

'And yet she and Jackson . . .'

'She is greedy and Jackson spends money on her. They both know the danger they run and their affair is more than discreet, so discreet no one, except the police, know about it.'

'So you could say Jackson is playing with dynamite?'

Gritten's smile broadened.

'That, Mrs. Rolfe, is an understatement.'

She got to her feet.

'Thank you. You have been more than helpful. What do I owe you?'

Gritten levered himself out of his chair.

'Mrs. Rolfe, I have read about you. If you will pardon me, it seems that you are what my American friends call a tough cookie. Anything I have told you that can fix Jackson is for free. You have my best wishes, but please remember that Jackson is also a tough cookie. If you need help, I am entirely at your service.'

'I won't need help, Mr. Gritten, but thank you for the offer.' Then flashing on her most charming smile, she left the office and not bothering to wait for the elevator, she ran down the stairs.

On her way back to the hotel, she glanced at her watch. The time was 16.20. She thought of the long hours ahead of her before confronting Jackson.

If only she wasn't so alone! If only she had someone to help her pass the hours until the morning. She must take no

76

risks. She would stay in her suite, have a lonely dinner on the terrace and take two sleeping pills for company.

She smiled bitterly. One of the richest women in the world and alone!

At 09.00 the following morning, Hinkle appeared with the service trolly.

'I trust you slept well, madame,' he said as he poured the coffee.

'Yes, thank you.' The two sleeping pills had given Helga an excellent sleep. She was feeling relaxed and her mind was very alert. 'I am sure you will be glad to get home, Hinkle.'

'Yes, madame. I find hotel life disagreeable.'

'Did Mr. Rolfe have a good night?'

'Apparently. He is under sedation, madame.'

She stirred her coffee.

'You saw Jones?'

Hinkle's face darkened.

'Yes, madame. He will be ready to travel after lunch.'

Casually, she said, 'He seems to be intelligent.'

'It would appear so.' Hinkle's voice conveyed his disapproval. 'He has, of course, a lot to learn.'

So Dick – she was now thinking of him as Dick – had made no difficulties. She felt a surge of excitement.

'I have to go out this morning and I will lunch in the grill-room.'

'Everything will be packed, madame. I will take care of the hotel cheque. We will leave at 13.30.'

'You are a great comfort to me, Hinkle.' She smiled fondly at him.

'It is good of you to say so, madame. I have already packed Mr. Rolfe's clothes and papers.' Hinkle paused. 'The red folder containing the letter to Mr. Winborn is missing.'

Helga felt a chill run over her. She should have thought of this possibility. Her mind worked swiftly. It was vital to her to retain Hinkle's trust. This was a sudden and dangerous situation. She had to keep him on her side.

'You have been good enough to tell me that you approve of me,' she said quietly, forcing herself to look directly at him. 'I can't tell you how grateful I am that you confided in me. I consider your confidence to be the act of a true friend, and Hinkle, I do need a friend.'

Hinkle's fat face softened. He bowed slightly and his eyes turned moist. She saw at once she was using the right approach.

'You advised me to read this letter. I did. Hinkle, I apologize. When you said Mr. Rolfe's mind was affected, I didn't believe you. I couldn't believe he has become a mental case. I saw him yesterday and I realized he has become a mental case. I now realize you are much wiser than I am. He looked at me with frightening hatred. I know people suffering from mental troubles turn on those they love the most. He and I have always been so close . . . so happy together. I have done everything I could do for him.' She put her hands to her face and caught her breath in a choked sob, willing the tears to come.

'Please, madame, don't distress yourself,' Hinkle said, his voice unsteady. 'May I say . . .'

She looked up. A tear rolled down her cheek.

'No, please don't, Hinkle. This is distressing for us both. You have been so kind to me. I read the letter. If Mr. Winborn reads it, my future is finished.' She lifted her hands in a gesture of despair. 'I know, as you know, if Mr. Rolfe had been normal he would never have written such a cruel, unjust letter. I took it.' She closed her eyes and another tear rolled. 'Dr. Levi tells me that Mr. Rolfe can't live much longer. I will keep the letter safely. If he recovers I will put the letter back among his papers, but if he dies – and pray God he won't and I pray God this dreadful mental illness will pass – then I intend to destroy the letter.' She looked directly at him. 'Tell me if I am doing wrong.'

'Madame,' Hinkle said huskily, 'I wouldn't have suggested you read that letter unless I hoped you would remove it. This is a sad and shocking thing. I am afraid Mr. Rolfe is a very sick man and what you have done is right. It will give me great satisfaction, madame, to continue to serve you.'

Helga turned away, frightened he would see the triumph that jumped into her eyes.

'Thank you, Hinkle,' she said huskily.

She waited until the door closed, then she drew in a long

deep breath. The cards were still falling for her. Trusting, kind Hinkle! She felt a pang of shame for deceiving him which she immediately dismissed.

Offence is better than defence.

Now for Jackson!

An hour later, she found parking in Ocean avenue and took the elevator to the fourth floor of Jackson's office block. She tapped on the frosted glass panel of his door, turned the handle and walked into a small office.

She was calm and the steel in her gave her fatalistic courage. Before long she would know if bluff and courage would defeat Jackson or if he was really the tough cookie that Gritten had said he was.

Facing her was a battered desk at which sat a young coloured girl with frizzy hair. She was wearing faded blue Levis and a man's crude coloured shirt, the tails knotted at her waist. She was reading a movie magazine and seeing Helga, her black eyes opened wide. Helga had deliberately dressed severely in a slate grey costume, relieved only by a string of pearls. Her cold sophistication and her hard, searching stare seemed to mesmerize the girl.

'Mr. Jackson,' Helga said, her voice snapping.

'Yeah, ma'm.'

The girl slid off her seat and opened a door on her right.

'You gotta customer,' she said into the room.

Helga brushed the girl aside and entered a shabby office only slightly larger than the outer office. She looked around, noting the two windows were grimy, the carpet threadbare, the steel filing cabinets badly scored.

Jackson who had been reading a racing sheet, jumped to his feet, dropping the sheet on the floor.

'Well, this is a surprise,' he said, forcing a grin.

Helga looked him over. This wasn't the immaculate blackmailer who had met her at the Pearl in the Oyster restaurant. This was Jackson in his working clothes; a shabby suit that needed pressing, a shirt with grubby cuffs and a food stain on the tie.

She waited until the girl had closed the door, then moving to a well worn leather chair by the desk, she sat down.

'I am rather rushed, Mr. Jackson,' she said. 'Mr. Rolfe and

I are leaving Nassau on the two o'clock flight. He has asked me to settle your account.'

Just for a moment, bewilderment showed in Jackson's eyes, then he recovered himself and laughed.

'That's swell of him, Mrs. Rolfe. I'm happy to hear he has made such a quick recovery.'

'How much does he owe you?'

Jackson's eyes narrowed.

'We had agreed about that, Mrs. Rolfe.'

'How much does he owe you?' Helga repeated.

'You agreed to pay me ten thousand dollars.'

'Mr. Rolfe will find that excessive.'

His face suddenly bleak, Jackson said, 'That doesn't concern me, Mrs. Rolfe.' Then the confident jeering smile appeared. 'That's for *you* to arrange with *him*, isn't it?'

Helga shrugged. She opened her bag and took out the ten one thousand dollar bills. She counted them so he could see them, then put them in her lap.

'If you will give me a receipt for ten thousand dollars for two day's work to give to Mr. Rolfe, I will pay you.'

His confident smile faded.

'So you are still trying to act tricky. I warned you about that, didn't I? That kite won't fly. I'll give you a receipt for one thousand dollars, the rest of the money is strictly between ourselves.' He paused, then leaning forward his eyes like stones, he asked, 'Have you got one of your fancy recorders in your bag?'

She nodded.

'I have, but it is not recording.' She took the tiny recorder from her bag. 'I brought it along so you could hear a recording I made yesterday. It is a conversation between myself and Dick Jones, your fink as you call him.'

Jackson stiffened.

'You may be a professional peeping Tom,' Helga went on, 'but you are a very amateur blackmailer.'

'You think so?' Jackson leaned forward, his face now an ugly snarling mask. 'Listen to me, baby, I've got you over a barrel! Give me that money or I'll take it!'

'You could be stupid enough to do just that.' She placed

the roll of bills on the desk. 'So you are not only a black-mailer, you are also a thief.'

Jackson reached for the money, then he paused and with-drew his hand. His eyes turned shifty as he stared at her.

'What are you cooking up?'

'A good question to use your own phrase,' Helga was be-ginning to enjoy herself. 'The bank has the numbers of these bills. The police, so I am told, are only waiting for you to make a slip and away goes your licence. I can prove this money belongs to me. Can you prove you didn't steal it? But go ahead and take it.' She paused, then said in a soft, deadly voice, 'Providing, of course, Mr. Jackson, you have the guts.'

For a long moment, he stared at the money, then at her. Blood rushed to his face.

'Right!' he said. 'That's it, baby! You have had your chance! The letter goes to Winborn!'

She laughed.

'Have you lost your nerve, Mr. Jackson? I am surprised. You are just a cheap phoney. How about the five hundred thousand you and your fink are going to share? Haven't you got the guts to fight for that?'

'Listen, you bitch . . .'

'No, Mr. Jackson, you listen to this,' and she switched on the recorder's playback.

As Dick Jones's voice came from the tiny speaker, Jackson stiffened. He remained like a stone man until the recording finished, then he snatched up the recorder and put it in his pocket.

'Don't panic, Mr. Jackson, I have a copy,' Helga said.

He glared at her, his good looks marred by vicious fury.

'Do you imagine anyone would believe a half-caste bas-tard's word against mine?'

'Don't you? You look worried.'

'Nice bluff, baby, but it won't work. You nearly had me going.' He forced a grin. 'Nearly, but not quite. No Judge would rule a tape recording. The first thing he would want to know is what was in the letter and how did you get hold of it from your husband's papers. You'd look pretty stupid wouldn't you, trying to explain. No, baby, you don't bluff me. Now let's cut out the smart tricks. I want clean ten one-thousand dollar bills and I want bearer bonds for five hundred thousand or else ...'

She studied him and realized he played a King to her Queen, but she wasn't dismayed, she still held the trump card.

'I did hope the tape would frighten you into giving me the letter, Mr. Jackson,' she said quietly. 'I see I have misjudged you.'

He stared suspiciously at her, then his face brightened and he laughed.

'It was a good try, baby. We all make mistakes. Now here's what you do ...'

'I know what I am going to do.' She leaned forward and stared fixedly at him. 'Something I don't want to do because, although you are a four letter man, Mr. Jackson, I don't wish you dead as I don't wish anyone dead.'

His eyes narrowed.

'Are you threatening me?'

'Regretfully, Mr. Jackson, you force me to blackmail you as you are blackmailing me.'

'What are you yakking about? Suppose you cut out this double talk? Here's what you do ...'

'I telephone Ed Lopez and tell him you are screwing his wife,' Helga said, speaking each word slowly and distinctly. 'I will tell him to contact Frank Gritten for proof. You have been watched, Mr. Jackson. That's what I will do unless you give me that letter immediately!'

Jackson reared back: blood left his face, his mouth turned slack and his eyes became glazed.

'If you have anything to hide, Mr. Jackson, never try blackmail,' Helga said. 'Give me that letter!'

Five minutes later, the red folder in her hand, she swept out of the office, past the staring young coloured girl and down the stairs to the street.

CHAPTER FIVE

NEVER had the sky looked so blue nor the sea so sparkling nor the crowds, swarming the beach, so happy and wonderful, Helga thought as she drove back to the hotel. She felt ten years younger, gayer and utterly reckless.

This best of generals didn't lose the battle! This was the second time that she had beaten a blackmailer to the punch, and what a punch she had given that sleezy creep! As she pulled up in a traffic block, she laughed aloud. An elderly man in a car alongside hers turned to stare at her. She gave him a flashing smile. He grinned shyly and looked away.

She could still see Jackson's craven face as he had given her the red folder, the letter and a photocopy. He had been shaking and sweating. She had thrown a thousand dollar bill at him, demanding a receipt. His hand had trembled so violently, he could scarcely write.

Snatching the receipt from him, she had said contemptuously, 'Have fun with your whore, Mr. Jackson. I won't talk, but sooner or later, someone will,' and she had left him.

That would sour his sordid romance, she thought and laughed again. The cards were still falling for her! In a few hours she would be flying home. Herman, in hospital, would be out of the way. She thought of Dick Jones, seeing his beauty and her heart began to race. She would have to handle him carefully, but he was young and full of sap. Seducing him would be an exciting experience and God! how she needed an exciting experience! For the first time that she could remember she was now desperately impatient to return home. Previously, the luxury villa with Herman hobbling around, had been like a coffin to her, but not now! With Dick there, opportunities there, Herman in hospital, she wouldn't even think of going to Switzerland. Winborn

83

had offered to advance her money. As soon as she returned to Paradise City, she would telephone him, telling him to put money in her account and debit the Swiss account.

She glanced at her watch. She had still two and a half hours before leaving Nassau. She decided she wouldn't have lunch in the sedate grill-room. In the mood for excitement, she would go to one of the West Indian restaurants. She didn't care that she was so severely dressed. She wanted fun and she was going to have fun!

Driving along the sea road, she pulled into the parking lot of the Riviera Tavern. The place was crowded with scantily dressed boys and girls. Music, with a terrific beat, blared from amplifiers.

A coloured man in white slid up to her.

'A table, lady?' There was a knowing grin on his face, telling her he had recognized her. She didn't care. She was in the mood to join the young, dancing.

'Yes, and a double vodka martini.'

'Lady, you will be happier in a bikini,' the man said. 'We sell them here. There's a changing room at the back.'

She laughed.

'Marvellous!'

Ten minutes later she was sitting at a table in a scarlet and white bikini, the drink before her. She was happily aware that her trim body compared more than favourably with those of the girls with their puppy fat and wobbly bottoms prancing in the centre of the room.

A tall, lean boy with shoulder length hair and a smiling self-assured expression, wearing only swim trunks, danced up to her.

'No, baby, no . . . you don't sit still in this joint. Come on! Come on! Turn it on! Shake it!'

She moved into the crowd with him and abandoned herself to the music. Some of the girls stared at her, but most of them seemed to accept her.

Jiggling before her, the boy said, 'You new around here, baby? I watch the chicks . . . the first time I've seen you.'

Chicks! She could have hugged him.

She was so elated and happy she didn't even want the

martini. When the music stopped, the boy said, 'You want to sharpen up on that tan, gorgeous. You swim?'

'Sort of . . .'

'Swim with me?'

'Why not?'

He grabbed her hand and ran with her across the sand and into the sea.

'You follow me, baby. I won't go far out,' he said.

She paused to watch him. A show off, she thought, no style and little speed. Letting him get well ahead of her, she cut into a racing dive, overtook him and went past him like a rocket. She swam a hundred yards or so, turned around and waited for him.

As he approached, she saw he was no longer happy.

'Say, who are you? Some athlete or something?' There was a sour note in his voice.

She realized her mistake. Men! Always wanting to be the top shots! She should have played helpless.

'Why didn't you say you could swim like that? You putting me on?'

The spark had gone. Would she ever learn?

'My drink is getting warm,' she said and turning, she swam back, leaving him staring after her.

To hell with men! she thought. Use them when you need them, drop them when you don't!

In the changing room, she rubbed herself dry, put on her dress, paid for her half-finished drink and decided, after all, to have a lonely lunch in the hotel grill-room. As she left she heard a girl say, 'What the hell does *she* want to barge in here for?'

And to hell with you! Helga thought.

She got in the Mini and stared through the dusty windshield. Well, at least she had been called a chick!

She had regained her high spirits by the time she reached the hotel. She was hungry and went straight to the grill-room. The Maitre d'hotel met her at the entrance, his expression serious.

'Excuse me, Mrs. Rolfe, they are asking for you at the desk.'

She stiffened and stared at him.

'Who?'

'I believe your man . . . Hinkle.'

Impatiently she looked at her watch. The time was 12.35.

'He must wait,' she said curtly. 'I want lunch.'

The Maitre d'hotel hesitated, then conducted her to a corner table. She ordered a crab salad and a half bottle of Chablis.

She was damned if anything was going to prevent her lunching, she told herself. Probably some stupid mix up with the luggage or something.

As she was finishing the crab salad, she saw Hinkle hovering in the doorway. One look at his face made her crumple her serviette and start to her feet.

Watched by the other people lunching, she joined Hinkle and they moved into the lobby.

'What is it?' she asked sharply.

'Mr. Rolfe, madame. I regret to tell you he is very poorly.'

She stared at him, her heart skipping a beat.

'Poorly? What do you mean?'

'Dr. Bellamy is with him. Would you come up with me, madame?'

A little chill ran through her, but aware that the staff and several tourists were watching, she walked with Hinkle to the elevator.

With the elevator attendant all ears, she couldn't ask questions until they began walking down the corridor.

'Won't we be leaving, Hinkle?' She could think of nothing else.

'I am afraid not, madame. Mr. Rolfe's relapse appears to be serious.'

Her triumph over Jackson, the exciting prospects of going home with Dick Jones vanished like a fist becoming a hand.

Goddamn Herman! she thought. But as soon as the thought passed through her mind, she felt ashamed. 'How would you like to be stricken with a drooling mouth, a useless arm and paralysed legs, you selfish thoughtless bitch,' she told herself.

She found Dr. Bellamy waiting for her. She had never seen such a worried looking man.

'Oh, Mrs. Rolfe, I have bad news. Mr. Rolfe is unfit to fly.'

'What's happened?'

'I regret to say that I don't know. Dr. Levi will be arriving in a few hours.'

'You don't know?' Helga snapped. 'Has he had another stroke . . . you must know!'

'He was under sedation. He seems to have drifted into a coma.'

'Seems? Surely you must know if he is in a coma or not?'

'The symptoms are puzzling, Mrs. Rolfe. Nurse Fairely became alerted when his breathing became light and his colour took on a bluish tinge. She sent for me. The heart action is strong, but the beat much slower.'

Helga stiffened.

'Is he dying?'

'I would say not, Mrs. Rolfe. It is an extraordinary change. I can't account for it. I have taken the precaution of giving him oxygen. My assistant is with him and will remain with him. Everything that can be done, will be done.'

'So there is no question of flying him home?'

'I am afraid not.'

'So we must wait for Dr. Levi?'

'Yes, Mrs. Rolfe.'

'And you can't suggest what has gone wrong?'

'I think it would be better to wait for Dr. Levi. Mr. Rolfe is his patient.'

Doctors! she thought.

'Well, we must wait then,' and not attempting to conceal her irritation, Helga left the room. She found Hinkle waiting in the corridor. 'I want to change, Hinkle, then we must talk. Would you give me fifteen minutes?'

'Certainly, madame.'

She entered her suite, her mind in a frustrated, bitter fury. Quickly she got out of the dress and put on a pyjama suit, then she lit a cigarette and began to pace up and down the big living room. All she could think of was Dick. She was still pacing when Hinkle tapped on the door.

'This fool of a doctor doesn't know what is wrong,' she said angrily as Hinkle came into the room. 'We have to wait for Dr. Levi. When did this happen?'

'A few minutes after you left, madame. Nurse Fairely called me and told me she had called Dr. Bellamy. He in his turn called Dr. Levi. Fortunately it was early enough for me to cancel the packing arrangements.'

She stubbed out her cigarette, exasperated.

'I'll go out of my mind if I have to stay much longer in this hotel!'

'That I can appreciate, madame. Perhaps Dr. Levi will give you some idea how long it will be.'

'I hope so!' She began to pace the room again. 'Well, all right, Hinkle, we must wait.'

'There is Jones to be thought of, madame,' Hinkle said, his voice dropping a tone.

As if she was thinking of anything else!

'Oh, yes.'

'Obviously we won't be requiring him now, madame. I suggest I see him and advise him to ask the hotel to re-employ him.'

No, Hinkle, she thought, nice and kind as you are, you don't make decisions.

'If Mr. Rolfe can travel in a few days, I still wish to give the boy his chance.' She kept moving around the room so she need not look at Hinkle who she was sure was registering disapproval. 'Let us wait until we hear what Dr. Levi has to say. Where is Jones?'

'I don't know, madame. I haven't seen him this morning. He had instructions to be in the lobby at 13.15. He is probably down there now, waiting.'

'All right, Hinkle. I'll send for you as soon as I have spoken to Dr. Levi.'

'Very well, madame,' and Hinkle withdrew.

Helga went immediately to the telephone and called the Hall porter.

'Is Dick Jones in the lobby?'

'Yes, Mrs. Rolfe. He is waiting for instructions.'

'Tell him to come to my suite, please.' She replaced the receiver and with an unsteady hand she lit yet another cigarette. What she wanted more than anything in the world, when Dick arrived, was to lead him into her bedroom, but she knew this was impossible. She would have to wait. She clenched her fists in frustrated fury. Wait! Wait! Wait! That's all she seemed to be doing with her life . . . waiting!

After knocking, Dick entered. He stood just inside the door, holding a shabby panama hat in both hands in front of him. He was wearing a cheap, crumpled grey linen suit, a white shirt and a dark blue string tie. Her eyes ran over him. In spite of his shabbiness he was still beautiful to look at and his big, fawn-like eyes gave her a sinking feeling.

'You have heard that Mr. Rolfe is too unwell to travel?' she said.

'Yes, ma'm.' A pause. 'I'm sorry.'

'Thank you, Dick.' She may as well get him used to her calling him by his first name. 'It is most unfortunate. It means I will have to postpone my trip.'

She was watching him closely and just for a brief moment the dark eyes lit up.

So you are pleased, little boy, she thought. All you are thinking about is your stupid motorbike. Well, I'll change all that. Soon, all you will be thinking about is me.

'I am waiting to hear what the doctor has to say. It could be that we will leave in three or four days. You may go home. When I want you, I will send for you.' She crossed to the table and took her purse from her handbag. 'Here is your week's salary. You are now a member of my staff. Do you understand?'

His liquid black eyes dwelt for a moment on the hundred dollar bill she was holding. His full lips moved into what could have been a smile, but it was instantly repressed.

'Yes, ma'm.'

She gave him the bill.

'You are to have no contact with Jackson, Dick. Is that understood?'

He flinched.

'Yes, ma'm.'

'All right. Now go home and wait.' She looked fixedly at him. 'Enjoy your bike while you can.'

He regarded her, then looked away. A flash of something in his eyes? She wondered, but she wasn't sure.

He opened the door, gave her a stiff little bow and stepped into the corridor, closing the door softly.

Could that flash in his eyes have been hatred? she won-dered. It was possible. She smiled. Opposition was always a challenge. She was confident his opposition wouldn't last long. This affair was going to be even more exciting than she had first imagined.

Like a red ball, the sun sank slowly into the sea. Long shadows crept up the beach. The palm trees were black against the rose and yellow sky. Happy people continued to laugh, shout, run, splash and scream. Cars continued to crawl along the sea road. To Nassau this was just another hot evening with a night to come of brilliant lights, music, dancing, the beat of drums and the shuffle of feet.

Helga sat on the terrace, only half aware of the night sounds, her mind occupied with the problem of her future.

'You sent for me, madame?'

Hinkle appeared at her side. He placed a silver tray on which stood a shaker and a glass on the table. He poured, then placed the glass within her reach.

'Sit down, Hinkle.'

'I would rather not, thank you madame.'

She turned on him.

'For God's sake, sit down!' Her voice was strident.

Startled, Hinkle pulled up a chair and sat on the edge of it.

'I'm sorry, Hinkle. You must forgive me. I didn't mean to shout at you. My nerves are shot.' She forced a smile.

'That is understandable, madame. Have you any news?'

'I have talked to Dr. Levi. Clever as he is and smooth as he is, I have come to the conclusion that he knows no more of what has happened to Mr. Rolfe than Dr. Bellamy does – which is exactly nothing!'

Hinkle's fat face registered shock.

'But surely, madame . . .'

'The fact is, Hinkle, these expensive and so called expert doctors won't admit when they are baffled. I am not taken in by Dr. Levi's vague talk. He says Mr. Rolfe is much worse – that is obvious – and he thinks the worsening is nothing to do with his stroke. This is something new. At least he is honest to admit he isn't sure what the new development can be. He talked vaguely about the symptoms resembling narcolepsy.

Doctors! How they love to hide behind their jargon! When I asked him what narcolepsy meant he said it is a curious condition – I am quoting him – which brings on uncontrollable attacks of sleep. When I asked him how this could have happened to Mr. Rolfe, he said he didn't know. He said Mr. Rolfe appeared to be in no immediate danger but it would be most unwise to fly him home. Arrangements are now being made to move him to the Nassau hospital.'

Hinkle moved uneasily.

'I am very sorry, madame. This is most distressing news. What does Dr. Levi propose?'

Helga lifted her hands in despair.

'He is calling in Dr. Bernstein who will fly from Berlin today.'

'There is, of course, no decision of when we can leave here?'

'I wish to God there was. No, Hinkle, we must wait.'

Hinkle, his face gloomy, got to his feet.

'Very well, madame. Will you be dining here?'

'I think I will ... on the terrace. Dr. Levi wanted me to dine with him but I have had enough of doctors for tonight.' She looked up at him. 'Give me one of your lovely omelettes.'

His face lit up.

'That will be a pleasure, madame.'

'Still no news of Miss Sheila?'

He shook his head.

'No, madame, but the mail, these days, is very unreliable.'

An hour later, Helga watched Herman's removal to the hospital. Dr. Levi, Dr. Bellamy and his assistant, two interns, two stretcher men and Nurse Fairely fussed around the inert body as it was carried to the elevator.

One of the richest and most powerful men in the world, she thought, now a sleeping, half-dead body but which still commanded the V.I.P. treatment.

'Leave all this to me,' Dr. Levi said in his deferential voice. 'Should any change occur I will let you know immediately. You must not worry. Once we get this extraordinary change in him diagnosed, I feel confident there will be a recovery.'

Words! Words! Words!

'Thank you,' she said.

How much better it would be, she thought, as she watched the elevator descend from sight, if he had said there was no hope: better for Herman: much, much better for her.

The rest of the evening was a dreary, depressing repetition of the previous evenings. She ate the omelette, praised it and then sat on the terrace, listening to the people still on the beach, enjoying themselves. The hours dragged. She tried to read a book, but it failed to interest her. She thought of Dick. What was he doing now? Rushing along the roads on his motorbike? Had he a girl? Was the girl clinging to him on the back of the bike? If it hadn't been for Herman's new and mysterious illness, the boy, Hinkle and she would, at this moment, be at the villa in Paradise City.

Dr. Levi had said he could give her no idea when it would be safe to fly Herman home. So she was stuck in this hotel, alone, until this goddamn doctor made up his goddamn mind! It could be days or even months!

Suddenly she realized she was wallowing in self pity. She pulled herself together. She was not going to just sit here, pitying herself, prepared to accept a long, lonely wait either for Herman to die or for him to be taken home. She must do something! She would do something!

Her eyes narrowed as she thought. She would have to remain in Nassau. This was something she had to accept and now wanted to accept because Dick was here. But that didn't mean she had to stay in this stiffling hotel, watched and talked about. Her active brain began to race. If she could find a small villa! Frowning, she saw a problem. Hinkle! She had gained his trust. She must be very careful to keep that trust. She knew Hinkle was longing to return to the Paradise City villa. She knew how he hated hotel life. She sat still, a cigarette between her slim fingers, as she thought. A villa with Dick! A villa without Hinkle! This was the solution! Keep thinking, she told herself, the solution will come if I keep thinking.

The buzz of the telephone startled her. Impatiently she went into the living room.

'Who is it?'

'Mr. Winborn, Mrs. Rolfe, calling from New York.'

'Put him on.'

'Mrs. Rolfe, Dr. Levi has telephoned me.' Winborn's voice, cold and polite came on the line. 'It seems that Mr. Rolfe has had a relapse. I am exceedingly sorry. It is a puzzling business, isn't it?'

'Yes. Dr. Levi is going to consult Dr. Bernstein.'

'So I understand. I called to know if there is anything I can do for you.'

'I won't be going to Switzerland. Perhaps you could arrange for me to be able to cash cheques here?'

'Certainly, Mrs. Rolfe. I will make the necessary arrangements ... say five thousand a week?'

'That will be more than ample.'

How easy it was to spend other people's money, she thought. If the money had been his, he wouldn't have thought in terms of five thousand dollars a week.

'You didn't find a letter for me then, Mrs. Rolfe?'

'I would have called you if I had.'

'Odd, isn't it? Nurse Fairely said Mr. Rolfe was so persistent.'

'Most odd.'

Go on talking, Helga thought, you're not as smart as you think.

A long pause, then he said, 'Well, please keep me informed. Good night, Mrs. Rolfe,' and he hung up.

Helga looked at her watch. The time was 23.25. She wondered if she should take sleeping pills. Why not? Sleep shut away her loneliness. She went into the bathroom. Half an hour later, she was dreaming that Dick was lying beside her. It was an erotic, wonderful dream and when she woke to find the sun coming through the blinds, she felt relaxed and refreshed.

She was dressed when Hinkle brought her her coffee.

'I'll call the hospital,' she said as Hinkle poured the coffee.

'There is no change, Mrs. Rolfe,' Dr. Bellamy's assistant told her.

As she hung up, she looked at Hinkle and shook her head. 'No change.'

'Let us hope when the other doctor arrives ...'

'Yes.'

When he had gone, Helga went down to the lobby and asked the Hall porter who was the best real estate agent in town. He gave her a name and directions and taking her Mini, she drove to the agency.

William Mason, the estate agent, was a young, cheerful looking Englishman who gave her a warm welcome. He said he was sorry to read about Mr. Rolfe's illness and he offered his best hopes for a speedy recovery.

'I am told there is difficulty in renting a furnished villa, Mr. Mason,' Helga said. 'My major-domo has made inquiries and everything seems to be taken. I don't know how long I will have to remain in Nassau, but I must have a furnished place. I can't continue to stay at my hotel.'

'I can well understand that, Mrs. Rolfe, but I regret I have nothing suitable for you. I can assure you, to save you wasting your time, that there is nothing the other agents could offer you either. The big villas have been snapped up.'

'Haven't you something small? Now my husband is in hospital, I don't need anything large.'

'Well, yes, I have something very small, but I don't think it would be suitable for you, Mrs. Rolfe. It has only one bedroom. It is a gem of a place, but tiny.'

Her heart began to beat fast with excitement.

'I would only want it for myself. My servant would come in daily.'

Mason beamed.

'Well then, perhaps you would like to see it. It is expensive and very isolated, but it is really nice.'

'Can I see it now?'

The tiny villa was exactly what Helga wanted. Completely isolated, with a quarter of a mile of private, screened beach, it had a big covered terrace which led into an enormous living and dining room, two bathrooms, an elaborately equipped kitchen, a big swimming pool with a covered Barbecue, a bar and up a steep flight of stairs a bedroom nearly as big as the living room. It was immacuately furnished throughout and it seemed to her everything was brand new.

'But this is wonderful!' she exclaimed. 'This is just what I want.'

'The rent is three thousand dollars a month. I have tried to get it reduced, but the owner won't budge.' Mason smiled at her. 'In confidence, Mrs. Rolfe, this is a wealthy man's love nest. As you can see nothing has been spared in the way of luxury. A woman comes in every day to clean. Unhappily there was a motor accident and the lady was killed. My client hasn't been near the place since. This is the only reason why it is to rent.'

A love nest!

Helga smiled. What a love nest! Again the cards were falling her way.

'I'll take it for a month,' she said. 'When can I move in?'

'As soon as the agreement is signed.' Mason looked slightly startled at her quick decision. 'Will you need the cleaning woman?'

'No ... I have my own servant. You mean I can move in tomorrow?'

'Certainly, Mrs. Rolfe. It will be two thousand dollars paid in advance and the agreement signed, then it is yours.'

'The telephone is connected?'

'Yes, no problem.'

'Then let us return to your office and I will sign.'

Driving back to the hotel, Helga's mind was busy. First, she would have to handle Hinkle, then she would have to get hold of Dick. In spite of her impatience to have Dick on her own, she would have to wait (this goddamn waiting again!) until Dr. Bernstein had arrived and had seen Herman. She would have to wait until Hinkle left.

Back at the hotel, she found Hinkle sitting on the second terrace reading John Locke's essays.

She sat beside him, putting her hand on his arm to prevent him from rising.

'I've been thinking, Hinkle,' she said. 'It is unnecessary for both of us to remain here. I am worried about the villa. If Mr. Rolfe can return, I want the place ready for him. You know what the servants are like without your supervision. They do nothing. The gardeners also will be doing nothing. We have experienced this before when you came to

Switzerland with Mr. Rolfe. I have to stay as much as I dislike it, but I want you to go back and make sure everything is immaculate when Mr. Rolfe returns.'

Hinkle's eyes lit up.

'But I can't do that, madame,' he said without much conviction. 'Who will look after you? No, madame, I would worry about you.'

She forced a laugh.

'Kind Hinkle! Surely you know me well enough by now to know I can look after myself. The hotel service is really very good. I know you hate sitting around like this. There are so many things to attend to at home. Wouldn't it be a wonderful opportunity to have Mr. Rolfe's study re-decorated? You have so often said how it needs a face lift and while he is in bed, you could have it done. So please leave tomorrow and make a start.'

Hinkle beamed.

'Well, yes, madame, I have long wanted to refurbish Mr. Rolfe's study. Yes, if you really think you could manage, it would be an opportunity.'

It was as easy as that.

Helga had little idea how she passed the rest of the day or the following morning. Her nerves were stretched to breaking point. It was only her steel control that kept her from screaming at the staff, at Hinkle, at Dr. Levi and Dr. Bernstein.

She held on because she was sure she had a retreat and in a day's time she would have Dick with her.

Before leaving, Hinkle had said kind things to her. She forced herself to say nice things to him. She could see how relieved he was to go, but she didn't envy him. Her life, she told herself, would begin when he had gone. From her living room window, she watched him get into the Rolls which she assured him she didn't need. As he drove away, she heaved a sigh of relief: one less pair of eyes to watch her.

Dr. Levi brought Dr. Bernstein to see her in the evening. Dr. Bernstein was a short, excessively fat man. She disliked him on sight. He spoke with a heavy German accent and waved pudgy hands while he talked.

In spite of his authority, his obvious confidence in himself, Helga, who was a good judge of men, realized after a few minutes that he was as baffled as Dr. Levi.

'The stroke, of course as Dr. Levi has told you, was massive,' Bernstein said. 'It has done damage, but, let us hope, not irreparable damage. This relapse could possibly be the reaction of an over-taxed heart. I wouldn't like to go further than this, Madame Rolfe. In fact until I have made various tests, it would be better not to go into details. I will observe the patient. It will take time.'

Bored with this fat, little man, Helga said, 'So you don't know what has happened? You have to make tests and you may find out. Is that the position?'

He looked at her, his eyes snapping.

'You can rely on me to make a searching examination, Madame Rolfe. This is an unusual case.'

She nodded, then turned to Dr. Levi.

'I am moving from here, doctor. Here is my new telephone number.' She gave him a card. 'Please keep in touch with me.'

'Of course, Mrs. Rolfe.'

Turning to Dr. Bernstein who was frowning, she said, 'You can give me no idea when my husband can go home?'

'An idea?' He lifted his heavy eyebrows. 'Certainly not. It is far too soon to think of air travel. Much will depend on the results of the tests.'

That night she had to take three sleeping pills before she slept. Tomorrow, she told herself, as she lay waiting for sleep, her life would begin.

Waking, she reviewed the coming day. Hinkle had gone. Herman was in the Nassau hospital for an unspecified time. Winborn was safely in New York. She had a love nest! There was no need to wait any longer. Now for Dick!

She frowned. But how was she to contact him? Her first impulse was to get in the Mini and drive to the broken-down bungalow and collect him, but she realized at once that the wife of one of the richest men in the world couldn't do that. She could tell the Hall porter she wanted to see Dick Jones. That too could be dangerous. Why should she want to contact a half-caste boy? The Hall porter would wonder.

Goddamn it! she thought. Must my life always be so complicated?

She had to be careful. She had to avoid gossip. So she lay in bed and thought. It irritated her to realize when one had something to conceal one had to cover one's tracks, continually look over one's shoulder and be cautious, and 'caution' was a word she loathed.

Then she thought of Frank Gritten.

She reached for the telephone and called his number.

'This is Mrs. Rolfe, Mr. Gritten,' she said when he came on the line. 'Thank you again for what you did for me.'

'I hope you were successful,' Gritten said.

'I was. You were good enough to say you would help me if I needed help.'

'I am at your service, Mrs. Rolfe.'

'I want to get in touch with an ex-servant of my hotel. His name is Dick Jones and he lives at 1150 North Beach road. Could you have a message sent to him to meet me at the Riviera Tavern at three o'clock this afternoon?'

There was a long pause. She could imagine Gritten puffing at his pipe. Then he said, 'That's no problem, Mrs. Rolfe.' Another pause. 'Would you like me to accompany you when you meet Jones?'

Startled, Helga said, 'What on earth for?'

'Jones is a J.D., Mrs. Rolfe. He served a year in a reform school when he was twelve years old. I suggest he isn't the type you should meet without someone like me with you.'

Helga stared into space. She saw the boy, saw his beauty, his fawn-like eyes.

'You surprise me, Mr. Gritten. Has he been in trouble since then?'

'No, Mrs. Rolfe, but all the same, once in trouble, always in trouble.'

'Isn't that being rather cynical, Mr. Gritten?'

'I am an ex-cop. One becomes cynical. We have a very high record here of J.D.'s. Most of them land up in jail. Do you still want to meet Jones now you know more about him?'

She didn't hesitate.

'Of course.' There was a snap in her voice. 'Please arrange it for me. Three o'clock at the Riviera Tavern.'

'All right, Mrs. Rolfe.'

'And thank you for not asking questions.'

He laughed.

'If there is anything else I can do, it will be my privilege.'

She thanked him and hung up. Was she being utterly reckless and stupid?

She thought of the boy and her heart began to race.

I can be too cautious, she thought. I have him where I want him. I am glad Gritten told me he has been in trouble. That means he will be more ready to do what I want. He will know I could get him into very serious trouble with that tape.

She relaxed back in her chair.

To hell with caution! She wanted a man, so she was going to have a man!

She enjoyed her lunch in the grill-room, knowing it was the last time she would eat there. After lunch, she saw the hotel manager and arranged for her cheque to be ready the following morning. He said how much he regretted that she was leaving the hotel and how much pleasure it had given him and his staff to serve her. She said the appropriate things.

A few minutes to 15.00, she drove to the Riviera Tavern. As she pulled into the parking lot she saw a group of scantily dressed young people surrounding an Electra Glide motorcycle. There were more girls than boys. The girls were chattering and squealing like a flock of parakeets: the boys silent and envious.

Astride the motorcycle was Dick Jones. For a moment she didn't recognize him. He was wearing a gondolier's straw hat with a red ribbon. The hat was tilted sideways, giving him a cheeky, sexy look. He wore only a pair of skin tight red trousers. Around his neck was a thick, gilt chain from which hung a replica of a tiny human skull, carved from bone.

Was this his off-duty gear? Helga wondered or had her money bought this finery? He was certainly a brash, handsome-looking little animal, she thought. No wonder the girls were swarming around him and the glittering white and red motor-cycle was impressive.

She sat watching, a cigarette between her fingers. Suddenly Dick seemed to become aware of being watched. He looked sharply at her and their eyes met. Purposely, Helga gave him her cold, steel hard stare.

His happy expression, his wide smile, revealing perfect teeth, faded. He straightened his hat and said something to the group around him.

They all stopped chattering and turned to stare at Helga who stared back at them. Then they broke up and all ran back to the Tavern, giggling and laughing: the boys shouting . . . all but one.

In the group Helga hadn't noticed this particular girl, but the moment the girl became isolated as she stood by the motor-cycle she seemed to Helga to be larger than life.

Around twenty-two or -three, this girl was well above average height and as she stood sideways on to Helga there seemed nothing of her: tiny breasts, no rear, long legs. Her hair that reached to her waist was tinted Venetian red. Helga thought she would probably be a mousy blonde before she had tinted her hair. The girl was wearing a grubby white T-shirt and tight, sun-bleached Levis with rabbit fur around the cuffs. All this Helga took in in one searching stare, then she looked at the girl's face. She felt a little pang of uneasiness: a strong face without being hard: a short nose, a wide, firm mouth and big eyes: no beauty, but by God! Helga thought, she was arresting: not like the other stupid puppy girls who had run away.

The girl continued to stare at her until Dick spoke to her. Then she shrugged and walked away with long, graceful strides, her head held high.

Getting off his motorcycle, removing his hat, Dick approached the Mini.

Helga saw the group of youngsters now standing in the shade of the restaurant's veranda. They were watching. This was a mistake, she told herself, to meet him here, but she didn't give a damn.

He came up to her and gave a stiff little bow.

Her voice cold and hard, she said, 'Do you know the Blue Heron villa, Dick?'

'Yes, ma'm.' His eyes were shifty.

'I have rented it. You will begin work tomorrow morning. It will be your job to keep it clean. Do you understand?'

He stared at her, then nodded.

'Can you cook?'

His eyes widened.

'Cook? Well no, ma'm. I can't cook.'

'It doesn't matter. Your hours will be from eighty-thirty until seven in the evening.'

He twisted his hat in his hands, looking away from her.

'Did you hear what I said?' Helga snapped.

He stiffened, then nodded.

'I will not have you nodding at me, Dick! You will say yes or no!'

'Yes, m'am.'

She regarded him as he stood in the hot sun, looking down, not meeting her eyes, his hands fidgeting with his hat, his expression sullen.

'Listen to me, Dick! I am doing you a favour! If I gave that tape to the police, with your record, you would be in serious trouble. You understand that?'

He flinched, then nodded.

'Yes, ma'm, and thank you, ma'm.'

She tried to resist asking the question, but burning curiosity proved too much for her.

'Who was that girl?'

His fawn like eyes widened.

'What girl, ma'm?'

'The girl with the red hair.'

'That's Terry, ma'm.'

'Terry . . . what is her other name?'

'Terry Shields, ma'm.'

Helga felt a wave of impatience run through her. Why should she have asked? She might have known the girl's name would mean nothing to her.

'Then tomorrow at eight-thirty. I expect you to be punctual, Dick.'

His eyes shifted.

'Yes, ma'm.'

'All right. Now go along and play with your friends.'

She started the car's motor and without looking at him she drove past the restaurant. The girls and the boys were watching her, but she didn't see Terry Shields. Was this girl Dick's special? She had stood so possessively by him when the others had run off. She had stared at her with hostility until Dick had spoken to her.

Competition?

Helga smiled.

She had no fear of competition. Dick would do as she told him: he had no alternative.

She would pack a bag and spend the night in the love nest, getting the feel of the atmosphere. There were things to buy. Milk, coffee, vodka . . . even toilet rolls. She must make a list. It was a long time since she had had fun. It was a long time since she had been in a Self-service store. It was also a long time since she had had a man in her bed. She had been patient. She had waited and waited and waited.

Tomorrow couldn't come fast enough!

CHAPTER SIX

HELGA pushed the market cart down the aisle stacked with canned food. It was years since she had done this and she realized what she had been missing. Before she married Herman, she had always had a sandwich desk lunch and gone out in the evenings.

She watched women putting cans into their carts, staring at the prices, rejecting one can, taking another. This was another world to her: not the magic world in which Herman Rolfe lived, but a more exciting world of 'Can I afford this! Should I splash out on that?' Lulled by Herman's money, this was a world she had forgotten.

She had a compulsive urge to buy. There were so many cans on the shelves with attractive labels that tempted her: red beans, chili con carne, lobster tails, ravioli. Then there were packets of various soups, ham ready cut and so on.

She was like a first ever tourist gaping at the wonders of Rome. She kept filling her cart, happier than she could remember and when she reached the meat and poultry counter, she took a T-bone steak and was reaching for a chicken when she realized she had no idea how to cook them nor did Dick. So she reluctantly put them back and moved to the counter that displayed the 'Heat and eat' foods.

She bought more than she wanted, but it was fun and she had plenty of money. She bought four bottles of Vodka and three martini, a pack of beer and whisky.

She loved standing in a queue, waiting for the goods to be checked. She felt in touch with people for the first time in years. Finally, she wheeled the cart to the Mini and loaded her purchases on the back seat.

Returning to the hotel, she asked the Hall porter to have her clothes packed.

'I will be in tomorrow morning,' she said. 'I won't be in tonight.'

'Certainly, madame. There is a cable just come in for your man, Hinkle.'

'Give it to me. I will be speaking to him.'

In her suite, she read the cable. The message was brief and from Paris.

Impossible to come to Nassau. Daddy will survive. He always does. Sheila.

The cards were still falling her way, Helga thought. She had been worrying about Herman's daughter. To have her here would have been embarrassing, but she was a little shocked at the girl's callousness.

She put the cable in an envelope and addressed it to Hinkle at the Paradise City villa, then she packed an overnight bag, not forgetting two bikini swim suits, a beach wrap and sandals. She then called down to the Hall porter to send someone to take the bag to the car and ten minutes later she was driving to the Blue Heron villa.

Putting the Mini into the four car garage, she unlocked the front door and entered the big living room. She looked around. Mr. Mason, the estate agent, had paid tribute to her wealth. Roses, carnations and orchids were tastefully arranged in various vases. His card, on which was written: *Have a pleasant stay,* lay on one of the tables.

Nice man! she thought and going over to the French windows, she threw them open and wandered out on to the terrace.

This was just what she had hoped for, she thought. She made a tour of the villa, carried her suitcase up to the bedroom and put on a bikini. The time was now 17.36. There was time for a swim, then she would unpack the groceries, make herself a drink, turn on the Hi-fi set and spend the rest of the evening dreaming of tomorrow.

She delighted in having all this wonderful beach entirely to herself. As she returned from her swim, she heard the telephone bell ringing. She ran into the living room and picked up the receiver.

'I hope I don't disturb you, Mrs. Rolfe.' She recognized Dr. Levi's voice.

'No, of course not. How is my husband?'

'His condition is the same. It is most puzzling. I can assure you that he is in no danger, but until he comes out of this strange coma, Dr. Bernstein is unable to commence his tests.'

'And when will that be?' Helga asked impatiently.

'We don't know ... any moment or much longer. I thought I should tell you we are satisfied that you have nothing to worry about. We must just wait.' A pause, then he went on, 'Dr. Bernstein has a very busy practice and he is returning to Berlin tomorrow. I am afraid I just can't remain here with so many other patients needing my services. I will be returning to Paradise City tomorrow. Dr. Bellamy will alert us when Mr. Rolfe comes out of this coma.' Another pause. 'Needless to say both Dr. Bernstein and I have complete confidence in Dr. Bellamy.'

'Oh, very well. If there is a change please tell Dr. Bellamy to call me.'

'That will be done of course, Mrs. Rolfe.'

She replaced the receiver, shrugging. For some minutes she thought of her husband, then with a grimace, she put him out of her mind and going to the garage she carried in the groceries and the drink, making two trips, but enjoying it.

Mr. Mason had turned on the refrigerator so there was ice. She made herself a large vodka-martini and drank it while putting the groceries away.

For the first time in years she would now prepare her own dinner. She looked through the various 'Heat and eat' packs she had bought and decided on the goulash pack. She read the directions and put on a saucepan of water. Then she found a pack of dehydrated potatoes. Again she read the directions which seemed simple enough and finding another saucepan she half-filled it with water and put that on the second burner.

By the time the goulash and the potatoes were ready, she had drunk another vodka-martini and was feeling a little high. The potatoes were too sloppy, but the goulash smelt good. She served both from the saucepans on to a plate, then realized she hadn't set the table. By the time she found the cutlery and a serviette, salt and pepper, the food was cold, but it wasn't bad, she told herself. Not what she was used to and she giggled at the thought of Hinkle's horrified expression if he had walked in at this moment.

'Well, at least I won't starve,' she said aloud. 'This is fun!'

Leaving the debris of the meal in the sink for Dick to clear up when he arrived the following morning, she made herself another vodka-martini and went into the living room.

She turned on the Hi-fi set and found a station broadcasting strident jazz with heavy drum effects.

Sitting in a lounging chair she watched the sun dip into the sea and she stayed there until the moonlight turned the sea to silver. She was more relaxed than she had been for a long time.

Tomorrow, she thought. My first night in Nassau when I won't be alone.

She thought of Dick and her heart-beat quickened.

No boy of his age could resist the urge of sex. He might not want her, but she had experience enough to know how to arouse him. It would be over quickly: the young with their excitement and lack of control were like that, but after he had rested, the second time would be good.

Soon after 22.00, she turned off the radio, turned off the lights in the living room, locked the french windows and went up to the bedroom. She undressed, showered and putting on a shortie nightdress, she got into the king's sized bed. She had a view to the sea, lit by the moon. The night was hot, still and utterly quiet.

A love nest!

Her hands moved over her breasts and she smiled.

Tomorrow!

Helga woke with a start, frowned at the bedside clock, saw it was 07.20. For a moment or so she couldn't remember where she was, then looking around the big, luxury bedroom, she remembered. She wondered what the owner of this love nest looked like: what his lady friend had looked like. *There was a motor accident and the lady died.* Helga grimaced. Some people were unlucky. Poor man! Poor girl! She remembered her father's cliché: 'It's an ill wind . . .'

She took a quick shower, put on a white pyjama suit and

went down to the kitchen. She longed for a good cup of coffee, but coffee making proved difficult. She found an elaborate machine with tubes which she didn't understand. There was a vessel into which she put coffee. When the water began to boil, the goddamn thing exploded, scattering coffee grounds over the wall and the built-in cupboards.

She glared at the machine in frustrated fury. She was going to have coffee! She banged a saucepan of water on the burner and when the water began to boil, she ladled in two big spoonfuls of coffee. The sonofabitch promptly boiled over, messing up the whole stove.

She turned off the gas and surveyed the scene helplessly. What with last night's meal clogging the saucepans, the stains on the cupboards and the mess over the stove, she gave up. She hoped to God Dick could make coffee.

Going to the refrigerator, she broke out ice and made herself a stiff vodka-martini and immediately regained her spirits. Changing into a bikini she had a swim. As she swam, she told herself she would have to find some woman to do the laundry. Mr. Mason would be helpful.

She got back to the villa a few minutes before 08.30. In a few minutes Dick would appear. She hurriedly changed back to her pyjama suit, then turning on the radio to pop music, she flopped into a chair.

The early drink had made her light headed and she longed for a cup of coffee. She thought of Hinkle, now so far away: his tap on her door and perfect coffee served.

Another of her father's clichés came to mind: *you can't have your bun and your penny.*

She laughed. Well, so far the bun wasn't much!

She closed her eyes. The relaxing swim and the cocktail sent her into a light sleep. The voice of the radio announcer giving the news brought her awake with a start.

She looked at the clock on the over-mantel. It was 09.20. She stared at the clock, then looked at her watch, then she jumped to her feet.

'Dick?'

He must have come in quietly and was cleaning up in the kitchen. She fluffed up her hair, smoothed down her pyjama suit and walked into the kitchen.

'Dick?'

Her voice came back to her in silence.

Moving quickly she went over the villa, out on to the terrace, then returned to the living room.

He hadn't come!

Fury took hold of her. For some moments, she stood shaking, her fists clenched, her eyes blazing.

Okay, little boy, she thought. You don't get away with this! You little bastard! If it's the last thing I do, I'll fix you!

Then she heard the roar of an approaching motorcycle: a deep-throated roar that made her stiffen.

Here he comes, she thought. You little creep! I'll teach you to be late!

There was a squeal of brakes, then the engine died.

She stood there, waiting. Her heart was racing now, her hands damp. Well, he was here! She would tongue lash him and when he was sufficiently humble and frightened, she would take him up to the bedroom. She felt suddenly excited.

The front door bell rang.

She forced herself to wait. She must not let him know how eager she was. She waited until the bell rang again, then she walked into the hall and opened the front door.

She had experienced many shocks in her life, but this shock was like a vicious punch to her solar plexus, leaving her breathless, cold and unable to move.

The girl, called Terry Shields, her Venetian red hair glittering in the sunlight, stood on the front step. She was wearing the same gear as the previous day although the T-shirt had been washed.

She regarded Helga, her big green eyes impersonal, no expression on her face. Helga absorbed the shock. Again the steel in her served her.

'What do you want?' she demanded, her voice hard.

'Sorry to be late.' The girl had a soft, pleasant sounding voice. 'I got held up at the hospital.'

'Hospital? Has something happened?'

'Dick had an accident,' the girl said. 'I warned him the bike was too heavy for him. He's broken his arm.'

Helga drew in a long, deep breath of exasperation. God! she thought, nothing, will nothing go right for me?

'You had better come in.' She turned and walked into the living room and dropped into a lounging chair.

Terry came in, shutting the front door and she moved into the living room. Helga saw her give a quick glance around.

'Sit down!' Helga snapped impatiently. 'How did it happen?'

Terry chose an upright chair. She sat down, her knees close together, her hands in her lap.

'He skidded. The bike is too powerful for him.'

'And yet you ride it?'

Terry shrugged.

'Girls are more careful than boys.'

A wise and sensible remark, Helga thought.

'So he has broken his arm?'

'That's it.' Terry shrugged. 'He is worried about you. You've paid him to work for you. He is conscientious. He asked me to take over until he is well enough.'

Helga reached for a cigarette, stared at it, then lit it.

'Take over?'

'Clean . . . run the place. I can do it if you want me to.'

Helga thought of the mess in the kitchen, the unmade bed upstairs and her need of a cup of coffee.

'Dick gave me fifty bucks,' Terry went on. 'So it won't cost you anything and I can do with the money.'

'I want a cup of coffee,' Helga said. 'Can you make coffee?'

'Oh, sure.' Terry got to her feet, looked around and without being told, made her way into the kitchen.

Helga smoked two cigarettes. Goddamn it! she thought. So I sleep alone again tonight! A broken arm! You don't take a boy with a broken arm into your bed. So again she must wait! Her fists clenched. Would there ever be an end to this eternal waiting?

Terry came into the living room with a pot of coffee, cup and saucer, sugar and cream on a tray. She set the tray on a table close to Helga.

'That machine you were using for coffee,' she said, 'is for making tea.'

Helga felt a moment of inferior complex which she immediately shook off.

'Oh? Who uses a machine to make tea for God's sake?'

Saying nothing, Terry returned to the kitchen. Helga heard her beginning to clean up.

The coffee was excellent, just as good as Hinkle made for her. She drank two cups, then getting to her feet, she went into the kitchen. Terry had already cleaned the stove and was now washing the stains from the wall.

'What is your name?' Helga asked although she already knew.

'Terry Shields.' The girl didn't pause as she rinsed a cloth in the sink.

'All right, Terry, until Dick is well enough you can work here.'

Terry paused and looked directly at Helga who wished some kind of expression would light up the girl's face, but the expression remained wooden.

'Okay. Do you want me to cook?'

'Can you cook?'

'Most women can, can't they?'

'I will be lunching out every day,' Helga said preferring to ignore what the girl had said. 'I would like dinner: nothing elaborate.'

'Do you want to eat this junk in the cupboard?' Helga stared at her.

'Junk?'

'These "Heat and eat" packs.'

'What's the matter with them?' Helga demanded, now angry.

'Please yourself.' Terry shrugged and she scraped the rest of the goulash from the saucepan into the trash bin. 'If you want me to cook for you, give me some money to buy decent food.'

After a moment's hesitation, Helga went into the living room, found her purse, took from it four fifty-dollar bills and returning to the kitchen put the bills on the kitchen table.

'Go ahead. I'm going out now. You don't have to stay here all day. Fix the place and come back to cook dinner tonight. I like to eat at eight-thirty.'

'Okay.'

Helga felt this was the moment to exert her authority.

'I would prefer you to say, "Yes, Mrs. Rolfe," instead of "Okay".'

'Okay, Mrs. Rolfe.' Terry looked at the four fifty-dollar bills. 'Do you want to feed an army?' She flicked aside three of the bills. 'Fifty is enough.'

Helga picked up the remaining bills, feeling irritated.

'You seem competent, Terry.'

'If I had your money, I wouldn't need to be,' the girl said and began to clean one of the saucepans.

Helga stared at her, then as the girl paid her no attention, she went upstairs, changed into a green linen dress, took a beach bag with a wrap and a bikini in it and returned to the living room.

'I will be back about six,' she said. 'Lock up, please. I have a duplicate key. I expect you here around seven.'

'Okay, Mrs. Rolfe. Rest easy. I won't steal anything.'

'You will stop being insolent if you want to continue to work for me!' Helga snapped. 'I don't expect you to steal anything!'

Terry looked at her, her face expressionless.

'You won't be surprised, Mrs. Rolfe,' and she moved by Helga and went up the stairs to the bedroom.

For a long moment, Helga stood motionless, then with an impatient shrug, she went to the garage and started the Mini. As she drove to the Diamond Beach hotel, she considered the new situation.

Dick out of action and now this girl. She had to admit the girl intrigued her. From her she might learn more about Dick and she wanted to know more about him. She realized to her surprise that her sexual need had faded. She was lonely. This girl could provide a stop-gap until Dick was well enough to come to bed.

Her bags, carefully packed, were in the hotel's lobby. She paid her cheque, shook hands with the hotel manager, lavishly tipped the Hall porter and then accompanied by smiles and bows, she drove back towards the Blue Heron villa. She would unpack, she told herself, then drive to the Ocean Beach club and become a member. She just couldn't go on living here without company. From the club's brochure she had read in the hotel the club offered everything to pass time: there was a casino, a swimming pool, tennis, golf, dancing, bridge and high speed motorboats to hire.

The traffic was heavy and she was forced to crawl along the main sea road, but she was relaxed and didn't mind. Passing a big Self-service store, she saw Dick's mother standing at the bus stop, two big shopping bags at her feet.

Helga swerved into the bus stop and pulled up.

'Hello, Mrs. Jones,' she called. 'Can I give you a ride?'

The big fat woman's face broke into a beaming smile.

'That's a little car, ma'm and I guess I'm a big woman.' She came up to the car, leaning forward smiling at Helga.

'We'll manage.' Helga opened the off side door.

Mrs. Jones heaved her two shopping bags on to the back seat, then laboriously climbed into the front seat. The car sagged a little. As she closed the door, Mrs. Jones said, 'That's real nice of you, ma'm. Not many folk stop to give a lift. I guess my dogs are giving me gyp this morning.'

Dogs? Helga thought. Feet?

'My son has been telling me about your place, ma'm,' Mrs. Jones went on. 'He says it is fine and big and splendid. I told him he was a lucky boy to have a room like that.' She looked searchingly at Helga. 'Ma'm, I hope he is taking proper care of you. I told him he has to be conscientious. This is a chance of a lifetime, I told him. He knows. My boy is no fool. He knows when he is well off.'

Helga's mind raced.

'So he likes his room?' she said. 'I'm so glad.'

'Yes, ma'm. He described it. He even has a T.V. set.'

'He only began working this morning,' Helga said, fishing for information.

'That's right, but you remember, ma'm, he came to see you yesterday evening. He came right back to me and told me all about it. I thought he would stay home with me while he worked for you, but he explained you needed someone around all the time.'

'I have friends who visit me,' Helga said. 'Dick will be helpful.'

112

'That I can see, ma'm.' Mrs. Jones nodded. 'It's a fine chance for him.'

Helga's face was expressionless as she said, 'I would like your advice, Mrs. Jones. Dick did mention a girl friend ... Terry Shields. He suggested she might also help in the villa.'

For a brief moment, she took her eyes off the traffic and looked searchingly at the big, fat woman at her side. She saw the dark face become set and a heavy frown creased the forehead.

'That girl? A no-good white trash!' Mrs. Jones snapped. 'You have nothing to do with her, ma'm. Dick's a good boy, but he's sort of crazy in the head about this no-good girl. You keep him working, ma'm. You see he doesn't have too much free time. If he does, he'll go running after this no-good girl.'

'What makes you think she is no-good, Mrs. Jones?'

'If you had kids, ma'm, if you were a mother, ma'm, you would know what is a good girl and what is a no-good girl. I know. I've seen her. She's no-good.'

'You saw Dick last night?'

'Saw him? Why, sure, ma'm. I helped him pack so he could move into your fine house.' Mrs. Jones turned and looked sharply at Helga. 'He did arrive last night, didn't he?'

Helga hesitated, then said, 'Yes, he arrived.'

Mrs. Jones beamed.

'That's it, ma'm ... like I say, he is a good boy.'

Helga pulled up outside the broken down bungalow.

'Thank you, ma'm,' Mrs. Jones said. 'You're real nice and kind. You make my boy work, ma'm. He is willing but he needs telling.'

Helga watched the big woman stump up to her front door. weighed down by her two shopping bags, then she did a U-turn and headed back towards the Blue Heron villa.

As she drove, her mind was busy. This meeting with Dick's mother had been fortuitous. The cards were continuing to fall her way. So she was being taken for a sucker. Her lips moved into a hard smile. As Dick wasn't living at home, where was he living? She guessed he had moved in with Terry. The story of the broken arm was a lie. Helga put herself in Terry's place. Dick would have told Terry he had been forced to work for her (Helga). Terry probably realized that she (Helga) had designs on Dick. The broken arm was a way out. Again Helga smiled. Don't rush this, she told herself. She needed a lot of information before she could fix these two. No one played her for a sucker. In the past a number of people had tried and later, were sorry.

She found she was driving along Ocean avenue and on impulse, she slowed and drove into a parking lot.

She walked to Frank Gritten's office block. As she waited for the elevator, she opened her bag and took out her cigarette case. The descending cage reached the ground floor, the doors swished open and she found herself confronted by Harry Jackson, wearing his glamour suit.

He started and lost colour when he saw her.

'Hello, Mr. Jackson, how smart you look,' she said.

He moved by her.

'Hi, Mrs. Rolfe.' His voice was husky. 'How is it?'

She stepped into the elevator, still staring at him.

'Thank you ... fine. I hope you and Mrs. Lopez are still happy.'

She thumbed the fifth floor button and as Jackson rubbed the back of his hand across his lips, the elevator doors closed.

Frank Gritten was sitting at his desk, puffing at his pipe. He got to his feet as Helga was ushered in by his elderly secretary.

'Good morning, Mrs. Rolfe. Take a chair. Nice morning, isn't it?'

'Yes.' She lit her cigarette, sat down and went on, 'I want to use your service, Mr. Gritten. I suggest a thousand dollar retainer.'

Gritten nodded.

'That's what I am here for, Mrs. Rolfe. What do you want me to do?'

'I have hired Dick Jones who I have already spoken to you about to keep my rented villa in order. The Blue Heron villa,' Helga said, crossing her shapely legs. 'He should have arrived this morning, but instead, his girl friend, Terry Shields, turned up, riding his motor-cycle. She tells me Jones has had an accident and has broken his arm. As I have already paid him a hundred dollars, he asked this girl to act as his stand-in. I have talked to Jones's mother and she believes her son is not only living at my villa, but is working for me. I find all this odd and I admit it intrigues me. I don't like people lying to me. I want you to find out what Jones is doing, whether he did break his arm, where he is living and who this girl is. I want it all in depth, Mr. Gritten.'

Gritten looked thoughtfully at her, then nodded.

'Should be no problem, Mrs. Rolfe.'

'I will be interested to know why Jones went to reform school. I also want to know all about Terry Shields. In fact, Mr. Gritten, I want all this in depth.'

Gritten nodded, then smiled.

'You will have it in depth.'

Helga dropped a one-thousand-dollar bill on his desk, then got to her feet.

'And I want it fast, Mr. Gritten.'

'You will have it fast,' Gritten said and escorted her to the elevator.

When Helga got back to the Blue Heron villa she saw the Electra Glide motorcycle had gone. She drove into the garage and lugged out her three suitcases, unlocked the front door and carried the cases, one at a time, into the living room. It irritated her that there was no servant to do this chore for her, but she shrugged this off.

She inspected the villa and found it was immaculate. The kitchen was spick and span. Dragging a suitcase up the stairs, she found the bedroom and the bathroom also immaculate.

She spent the next hour unpacking and putting her clothes away. By the time she had finished it was 13.10 and she was hungry.

Should she go out? She went down to the kitchen and inspected the 'Heat and eat' packs. The chilli con carne pack carried an appetizing photo in colour of the finished dish. She decided to eat here instead of the bore of finding a small restaurant. This time the potatoes were a success and she enjoyed the meal. She was about to leave the cleaning up, but decided not to let Terry know she had eaten 'junk'. It took her a while to wash up and this irritated her, but she took care to restore the stove and the sink as she had found them.

She then went into the living room, stretched out on the big settee and did some thinking. Dick would have to be punished, she told herself. She must wait for Gritten's report. If the boy really imagined he could fool her, he was in for a shock.

Around 15.00, she left the villa and drove to the Ocean Beach club. The magic name of Rolfe swept away any sponsors or the entrance fee.

The secretary of the club, a fat little man with a beaming smile, said the club would be honoured to have her as a temporary member. He was sure she would find everything to her liking and he extolled the club's facilities.

'You will want to meet people, Mrs. Rolfe. I assure you you will be welcomed by everyone.'

He took her around the club, introducing her to the English members: the old and the over-fat, the men with veins of drinking raddling their faces, the women in odd hats who smiled suspiciously, but all anxious to welcome the wife of one of the world's richest men.

Helga hated them all, but she knew she just couldn't go on living alone in the villa and had to have contacts ... but what contacts!

She endured an English tea with sandwiches and plum cake, surrounded by kindly, yakking people who kept looking with greedy eyes at the trolley loaded with cream cakes.

She thought of Dick. If the little bastard had kept faith, she and he would be in the king's size bed right at this moment. She refused another cucumber sandwich.

'But they are so good, Mrs. Rolfe. With your beautiful figure, you don't have to worry about dieting.'

Stifled and utterly bored, she finally broke away. She noticed the men were looking with astonishment at her modest car. Rolls, Bentleys, Cadillacs surrounded the Mini.

She drove back to the villa. Remembering Herman, she called the hospital to be told there was still no change in his condition. The time was 18.15. She went up to her bedroom and put on a white pyjama suit, then going down to the living room, she mixed herself a vodka-martini. She listened to the T.V. news. The fluctuation of the dollar worried her. She thought of all the dollars she had in the Swiss account. She should have converted them into Swiss francs.

A few minutes before 19.00, she heard the roar of the approaching Electra Glide. The engine cut, then the front door opened.

Terry Shields came into the living room, carrying a paper sack.

'There you are, Terry,' Helga said, smiling. 'Thank you for cleaning up so well.'

The girl was wearing a blue short-sleeved shirt and dark blue stretch pants. Her hair looked damp as if she had been swimming.

'I got scampi,' she said. 'That okay for you?'

Helga regarded her. Again she was impressed by the strength of character that showed in her face. A no-good girl? She certainly didn't look no-good.

'Scampi? Yes . . . fine.' A pause, then she asked, 'How is Dick's arm?'

As Terry moved towards the kitchen, she said, 'I didn't ask him.'

Helga's mouth tightened. She finished her drink, then getting to her feet, she went to the kitchen door. Terry was unpacking the paper sack.

'How long have you known Dick?' she asked, leaning against the doorway.

'Long enough,' Terry said curtly. 'Do you like these grilled in their shells or in a sauce?'

'Whichever is the easiest,' Helga said impatiently.

The girl turned and looked at her, her face wooden.

'No good cooking is easy, Mrs. Rolfe,' she said. 'Say what you want and you'll get it.'

'Oh, in their shells . . . I'm not hungry.'

Terry dropped the scampi into a sieve and ran cold water over them.

'Is Dick your boy friend, Terry?' Helga asked.

Terry shook the scampi, then turned them out on to a cloth.

'You could say that.'

'And you? Where do you live?'

'I have a pad.'

'I am sure you have, but where?'

'North side.'

A long pause while Terry blotted the scampi dry. Helga was determined to persist.

'I was talking to Dick's mother this morning. She tells me he isn't living at home. Is he staying with you?'

Terry turned on the grill.

'Does it matter?' She picked up a pack of rice. 'Rice okay? You can have dehydrated potatoes if you want them.'

'I'll have rice.' A pause. 'I am asking you: is he staying with you?'

Terry poured rice into a cup.

'Are you that interested, Mrs. Rolfe?'

Helga controlled her rising temper.

'Oddly enough, Terry, I am. Is he living with you?'

Terry poured hot water into a saucepan and set it on a burner.

'Yes, he is staying with me and he screws me.'

Shocked, for a moment Helga was speechless. She abruptly realized, by questioning this girl, she was inviting insolence.

'I am not interested in your relations with him,' she said, her voice cold. 'I want to know where he is.'

Terry added salt to the water. She began to wash the rice.

'His mother said nothing about his breaking his arm,' Helga said through the silence.

Terry tipped the rice into the boiling water.

'Do you mind eating early, Mrs. Rolfe?' she said without looking at Helga. 'I have a date.'

'Did you hear what I said?' Helga snapped. 'I don't believe he has broken his arm!'

Terry began to lay the scampi on the grill.

'Do you like lemon juice, Mrs. Rolfe? Some people are allergic to lemon. If you don't dig lemon, there's tabasco.'

'Terry! Has he or has he not broken his arm?'

'If you want dinner, Mrs. Rolfe, could you let me get on with it? All this talk holds me up.'

Helga controlled herself with an effort. The calm, cold

118

effrontery of this girl was something she had never before experienced.

'I am asking you a question and I want an answer!' she said, her voice strident.

'It'll be ready in ten minutes, Mrs. Rolfe. Excuse me. I'll set the table.'

Side-stepping Helga, Terry went in to the living room.

Helga stood motionless, her hands into fists. She longed to rush into the living room, grab hold of this insolent little bitch and slap her face. Get hold of yourself. You're handling this like a moron.

She walked into the living room and not looking at Terry who was laying the table, she turned on the television set. A close up picture of a girl swam into focus on the screen. She seemed to be trying to swallow a microphone and her mouth was as big as a fire bucket. Her amplified, brash voice exploded into the room. Helga winced and turned down the sound.

Terry returned to the kitchen.

There was a long pause while the girl on the screen fought with the microphone and made noises like a cat on heat.

Terry returned, carrying a dish and a plate.

'It is all ready, Mrs. Rolfe. You haven't any wine. If you had told me, I would have got you some.'

Helga walked over to the neatly laid table and sat down.

'I'll get some tomorrow. This looks very good.' She surveyed the scampi, perfectly cooked and the bowl of rice. 'You seem to be a very good cook, Terry.'

'Well, if that's all, Mrs. Rolfe, I'll run along,' Terry said. 'I'll clear up tomorrow.'

Helga, now calm, now steel hard, began to peel one of the scampi.

'No, it is not all, Terry. Sit down.'

'I'm sorry, Mrs. Rolfe. I told you. I have a date.'

Helga spooned some rice on to her plate.

'Sit down!' She ate one of the scampi. 'Excellent.'

Terry was moving to the door.

'Terry! Did you hear what I said? Sit down!'

'Sorry, Mrs. Rolfe. I am late already.' She reached the door and opened it.

'Sit down!' Helga screamed at her. 'Unless you want to see your fancy boy in jail!'

Terry paused, then shrugging, her face expressionless, she came back into the room and dropped into a lounging chair.

'Score one,' Helga said to herself. 'So this little bastard does mean something to her!' She ate another scampi, squeezed lemon over her rice, wished there was a glass of Chablis to go with the meal.

'Did Dick tell you he is in trouble?' she asked, selecting another scampi. She forced her voice to sound calm.

'Say what you have to say, Mrs. Rolfe, and make it short,' Terry said indifferently. 'I have a date.'

'These scampi are very good,' Helga said, thinking, "I'll give this little bitch a taste of her own medicine." 'Is your date with Dick?'

'Why should you care, Mrs. Rolfe?'

A point to her, Helga thought. Be careful.

'Yes, Dick is in trouble,' she went on. 'Didn't you wonder how he managed to buy a motorbike costing over four-thousand dollars?'

The girl leaned back in the chair, crossing her long legs.

'That is his business. Only people with little to do stick their noses into other people's business.'

Another point to her, Helga thought, but I hold the trump card.

'He didn't tell you he stole a ring from me, sold it and with the proceeds bought the bike?' She shelled another scampi and squeezed more lemon.

Terry said nothing. She looked at her watch, then re-crossed her legs.

'Did you hear what I said?'

'Yes. Why should I care?'

'Don't you?'

'Is there anything else you have to say, Mrs. Rolfe?'

'Yes. Tell Dick that unless he is here by nine o'clock to-night, a police officer will pick him up and I will charge him with stealing my ring.'

Terry nodded and got to her feet.

'At nine o'clock? What would you want him for at that time, Mrs. Rolfe?'

Helga finished the last of the scampi.

'Oh, to clear up, Terry. Just run along and tell him.' She stared at the girl, steel in her eyes. 'Unless, of course, you want him to spend the night in jail.'

'Mrs. Rolfe, I will make a suggestion.' Terry groped in the hip pocket of her pants and took out two crumpled fifty dollar bills which she dropped on the floor. 'That's the money Dick owes you. You won't be seeing him nor me again. Now for the suggestion: when a middle-aged woman gets hot pants for a boy young enough to be her son, cold water helps. Go sit in a cold bath, Mrs. Rolfe,' and turning, she walked out of the room and out of the villa.

As she listened to the roar of the motorcycle fading into the distance, Helga stared down at the empty scampi shells as empty as she felt at this moment.

CHAPTER SEVEN

THE palm trees rustled in the slight breeze. Every now and then there came the sound of a soft thud as a coconut dropped. The faint roar of the traffic along the sea road blended with the swish of the sea, breaking on the beach.

Helga lay on the cushioned terrace chair. She had turned on the submerged lights in the big swimming pool, but had left off the terrace lights. The expanse of blue water, lit softly, made a soothing reflection on the terrace.

A middle-aged woman with hot pants.

The cruellest and the truest thing that had ever been said of her. A cigarette smouldered between her fingers. For as long as she could remember this sexual urge had tormented her: they had a word for it: nymphomania. She had imagined it was her own private and very special secret. Now this girl had ripped away the pretence. Thinking back into her past, Helga forced herself to admit the shaming fact that other people also knew, although they hadn't said so. The smiling waiters, the young, husky men, even the middle aged roués with whom she had spent an hour or so were even now probably talking about her.

'Strictly between you and me, old fella,' she imagined them saying, 'that Rolfe bitch is really keen. You know ... Herman Rolfe's wife. She drops on her back at the drop of a hat.'

Helga felt a cold shudder run through her. She knew men. She knew they couldn't resist boasting of their conquests. Why had she imagined – as she had done – they didn't talk and snigger about her?

Well, you have asked for it, she told herself. You have never had the guts to fight this thing. You could have gone to a Head shrinker if you had really wanted to make a fight of it. A Head shrinker? A crutch! No, that wasn't the way. She had to cure herself, and it still isn't too late!

This girl had jolted her to face the fact that she just must stop being promiscuous (and even as she told herself this, she remembered the times she had already made this empty promise). If only Herman would die! She would marry again, be free of all these dangerous sexual adventures. Herman's letter condemning her to the life of a nun was still in the hotel's safe. She would destroy it if he died, but if he recovered!

She closed her eyes.

If he recovered, her life would become unbearable. She remembered the hate in his eyes, his twisted mouth getting out the word: *bore!* which she knew meant whore. If he recovered she would have to leave him. She would find a job. She would find a husband with money. She...

Goddamn it! she thought. Face up to it! What man with important money would want to marry me at my age? But with sixty-million dollars the magic key to the world would be in her hands.

She thought of Dick Jones. She must have been out of her mind even to have thought of taking this callow boy into her bed. But it hurt that he seemed so desperate to keep out of her bed that he had invented the excuse of a broken arm. To hell with him! She had had yet another escape. Forget him! Let him fool around with Terry. But, and again a cold shiver ran through her: they would both be sniggering.

Let them snigger! That girl with her red hair! Admit it, Helga thought, she is impressive. She has character. She is wasted on a little creep like Dick.

She got to her feet and wandered around the swimming pool. Was this going to be her future life as long as Herman lived? Luxury and loneliness? She thought of the Ocean Beach club with all those awful English freaks with their greedy eyes fixed on the trolley of cream cakes and the men with their raddled faces and swollen bodies. If only Herman died! Then she would be free: the mistress of sixty-million dollars!

She became aware that the front door bell was ringing. She looked at her watch. The time was 20.40.

Was it Dick?

Had Terry given him her message and, scared of the police, he had come?

Even the thought of taking him into her bed now revolted her, but by God! she would vent her misery and fury on him! She would give him something by which to remember her!

She walked quickly across the living room as the bell rang again. Jerking open the door, her eyes snapping fire, she once again received a shock.

Instead of the fawn-eyed Dick, Frank Gritten stood on the doorstep, pipe in mouth, his grey suit ill-fitting, the centre button of the jacket straining against a generous paunch.

'Excuse me, Mrs. Rolfe.' He removed his pipe and raised his panama hat. 'I was on my way home and saw the lights. I have information for you, but if you would rather I came back tomorrow . . .'

She forced down her fury and managed to smile.

'Come in, Mr. Gritten. I was just going to have a drink. Will you join me?'

'Thank you.'

He followed her into the living room.

'This is comfortable, but lonely.'

'Yes.' She walked over to the cocktail cabinet. 'What would you like?'

'You are here alone, Mrs. Rolfe?'

She paused and looked at him.

'Yes.'

'Is that wise? You are very isolated.'

'What would you like to drink?' The snap in her voice told him she wasn't in the mood for advice.

'We policemen drink whisky, Mrs. Rolfe.'

She forced a laugh.

'I've read enough detective stories. I should know that.'

She made him a stiff whisky and soda, then fixed herself a vodka-martini.

'It's cooler outside.'

Carrying his drink, Gritten followed her on to the terrace

and when she flopped into her lounging chair, he sat beside her.

'I remember the owner of this villa, Mrs. Rolfe. He was unlucky.'

'So I have been told.' She sipped her drink, thinking it wasn't as good as the vodka-martinis Hinkle made for her. 'So you have information for me?'

'Yes. You said you wanted it fast.' Gritten lit his pipe, drank some of the whisky, nodded his approval, then went on, 'Dick Jones.' He paused to look at her. His blue eyes had the hard stare of a police officer. 'I am not only going to give you information, Mrs. Rolfe, but I am also going to offer you advice.'

She met the probing eyes with her steely stare.

'I am interested in facts, Mr. Gritten. I don't need advice!'

'That's the point.' Gritten puffed at his pipe, apparently unperturbed by the snap in her voice. 'I'll give you the facts, but in your present situation, Mrs. Rolfe, you also need advice.'

'Give me the facts!'

Gritten removed his pipe, regarded it, then tapped the glowing tobacco with his finger.

'You are a newcomer to Nassau and possibly to the West Indies. I have lived here for twenty years. You hired Jones to work for you. You probably thought he was a deserving boy whom you would like to help. You didn't take the precaution to speak to the police about him, and, Mrs. Rolfe, before you hire anyone here, it is essential either to take up references or consult the police.'

Helga sipped her drink, then set down the glass.

'Are you telling me I made a mistake hiring this boy?'

'Yes, Mrs. Rolfe, that's what I'm telling you. I told you Jones has been in trouble. He is the last servant you should employ as you live here so alone.'

Helga stiffened.

'For heaven's sake! A boy like that? Don't tell me he is a murderer?'

Gritten's expression remained serious as he shook his head.

'No, he is not that. At the age of twelve, he was sent to a reform school for stealing a chicken.'

Thoroughly irritated, Helga sat forward, her eyes snapping.

'Are you telling me that a twelve year old boy can be sent to a reform school for stealing one goddamn chicken? I've never heard of such a disgraceful thing! He was probably desperately hungry!'

Gritten removed his pipe, rubbed the bowl and then replaced it in his mouth.

'I was rather expecting you to say just that, Mrs. Rolfe, but then you don't know the West Indians. This is my point. The chicken wasn't eaten. It was used for a blood sacrifice.'

'A blood sacrifice? Is that such a crime?'

'Not to you perhaps, but let me explain. Some seven years ago, a Voodoo doctor came here from Haiti. You probably don't know what a Voodoo doctor is, Mrs. Rolfe. He is a man who has remarkable talents to make witchcraft. If he is a good man, he makes good magic. If he is an evil man he makes bad magic. This man – his name was Mala Mu – made bad magic. He started an extortion racket here. "You pay me so much or your husband, your wife or child will fall ill." That kind of thing. Few British residents here bother about the native quarter. The police have to. Voodoo is something they are very aware of and can't afford to ignore. Mala Mu employed Jones to steal chickens, dogs, cats and even a goat or two for his blood rituals. Finally the police arrested Mala Mu and also Jones.'

Helga finished her drink.

'I've never heard of such rubbish,' she said. 'Witchcraft . . . magic . . . blood rituals.' She made an impatient movement with her hands. 'I can understand ignorant natives believing such nonsense, but you . . . surely you of all people . . . can't believe such ignorant rubbish.'

Gritten regarded her calmly.

'I understand your reaction, Mrs. Rolfe. When I first came here, I thought like you that Voodoo was nonsense. I also believed that no man would walk on the moon. Now, being here for twenty years, I have a much broader outlook. I am satisfied that Voodoo not only exists, but is an extremely dangerous force. I can assure you that Jones is just as dangerous as Mala Mu was. He, by the way, died in jail. The police suspect that Jones learned a lot from Mala Mu and he is now practising witchcraft although they have no proof.'

This seemed to Helga to be so ridiculous that she lost patience with this placid, pipe smoking man.

'This is something I don't accept,' she said curtly. 'I suppose if you have lived for years in this exotic, sun-soaked place among superstitious coloured people you might believe in such nonsense as witchcraft, but I don't and never will!'

Gritten found his pipe had gone out. He re-lit it before saying. 'That's right, Mrs. Rolfe. As you have employed me, it is my job to give you the facts. It is up to you to accept or reject them. Now there is something that is bothering the police. Jones has become the owner of an expensive motor-bike. Chief Inspector Harrison who is in charge of the police here is wondering how a poor boy like Jones could find more than four thousand dollars to buy this bike. Blackmail goes hand-in-glove with Voodoo, Mrs. Rolfe.' Gritten paused and looked at her, his blue eyes probing. 'If Jones is blackmailing someone, the victim can rely on the police to keep his or her name secret. Harrison would like nothing better than to put Jones in a cell.'

God! Helga thought. The messes I get into!

Gritten waited, looking at her and when she said nothing, he went on, 'People are often reluctant to admit they are being blackmailed. This is understandable, but it does ham-per the police. Blackmail victims are always protected and are always treated as V.I.P.s.'

Helga hesitated. Should she tell this burly, pipe smoking man the whole sordid story? She wanted to but couldn't face confessing to him that she was a middle-aged woman with hot pants.

'I asked you, Mr. Gritten,' she said, using her cold steel voice, 'to find out if Jones had broken his arm, where he is now living and to give me information about this girl. Terry Shields. That was our terms of reference and what I am paying for. I have now decided not to employ Jones so if he happens to be a blackmailer and a Voodoo doctor, it is no concern of mine. Has he broken his arm?'

Gritten puffed at his pipe as he looked at her.

'Yes, Mrs. Rolfe, he has broken his arm. Late last night he got into a skid and took a bad fall.'

Helga felt suddenly deflated. So the broken arm hadn't been an excuse! Terry hadn't been lying. More important still, the boy hadn't made the excuse of a broken arm to keep out of her bed.

'And where is he staying?'

'Last night, he stayed at a beach hut owned by Harry Jackson, Mrs. Rolfe,' Gritten said, his police eyes watching her.

Startled, Helga somehow kept her face expressionless.

'How odd! Was he alone?'

'According to my operator who is still watching the hut, Jackson joined Jones around one o'clock last night. He left just after nine o'clock this morning. Jones is still in the hut.'

'The girl – Terry Shields wasn't there?'

'No, Mrs. Rolfe.'

Helga thought, then shrugged. She forced herself to show indifference which she didn't feel.

'Well, thank you, Mr. Gritten. I have one small problem. As I am not employing this boy, I am without a servant. Could you recommend someone? I won't be entertaining here so the cooking will be simple.'

Gritten rubbed the bowl of his pipe as he thought.

'You would be wise not to employ a West Indian, Mrs. Rolfe,' he finally said. 'The English woman who works for me has a sister who needs employment. Her name is Mrs. Joyce. Her husband was a fisherman. He was drowned in a storm last year. I can recommend her.'

'Then would you ask her to come tomorrow? I was paying Jones a hundred a week. Would that be all right for her?'

Gritten gaped at her. For the first time she had surprised him out of his calm.

'That is far too much, Mrs. Rolfe. Fifty would be more than enough.'

Too much? Helga thought, with all her money?

Impatiently, she said, 'I wish to pay her a hundred dollars a week. Money helps people. I like to help people.'

Gritten again gave her a hard cop stare.

'She will be delighted.'

128

'Then I think that is all, Mr. Gritten. Thank you for the information. The assignment – do you call it that – is now finished.'

Gritten brooded for a moment.

'There is the girl, Terry Shields. Do you still want a report on her?'

By now Helga was utterly sick of Dick Jones and Terry Shields. She wanted no more of them.

'I am no longer interested. Thank you for what you have done.'

Gritten leaned forward and tapped out the dead ash from his pipe into the ash tray.

'Then I owe you some money, Mrs. Rolfe.'

'I said your assignment is finished. You owe me nothing.' She forced a smile. 'Again my thanks for what you have done.'

Gritten got to his feet.

'Are you sure, Mrs. Rolfe, you don't want to check on this girl?'

Helga now longed to be alone. She had to control herself not to scream at him.

'No, thank you, Mr. Gritten. I no longer need your services.'

It was one of her impulsive decisions that she was to later regret.

Mrs. Joyce turned out to be more English than the English. She arrived on a bicycle which seemed to be buckling under her weight. She was a large woman, heavily corseted, around forty years of age, her hair tightly permed, her English complexion reminded Helga of a polished apple.

'Do you like tea, ducks?' she asked as soon as she had introduced herself. 'Or are you a coffee fiend?'

Startled, bewildered, Helga said she preferred coffee.

'I'm a tea drinker.' Mrs. Joyce beamed. 'It's an English habit. You just sit and rest yourself. I'll have a cup of coffee for you in a jiffy.'

For God's sake! Helga thought. What have I found now?

But the coffee was good and Mrs. Joyce's kind chatter amusing.

'Wonderful place, isn't it dear? But you must feel lonely. I miss my man. Us girls get lonely without our men. I read about your good husband. At least, he is alive. My Tom is just a memory to me, but a precious memory. He was a fine man. Would you like me to get lunch? Or would you like a nice bit of fish for supper?'

Helga said she would like dinner. She would be out for lunch.

'What a lovely figure you have, ducks,' Mrs. Joyce said admiringly. 'I've worked for other ladies. My! They just don't take care of their figures, but you ... honest, ducks, you should be proud!'

Slightly bewildered, Helga warmed to this woman. She felt in need of kindness.

'How nice of you to say that, Mrs. Joyce. You are right ... living alone, I get depressed. I suppose when one reaches forty-three and there is no man around, one does get depressed.'

'Forty-three? You're making yourself a liar, dear. You don't look a day older than thirty. My hubby used to say a woman is old as her roll in the hay.' She laughed, slapping her work worn hands together. 'My Tom was a proper caution. The things he used to say! but he was right. So long as you miss a man, you're not old.'

Helga suddenly relaxed, and smiling, she said, 'Do you ever want a man, Mrs. Joyce?'

The big woman grinned.

'Me? Why, ducks, that's what life is about, isn't it? When I get hot, I find a man. Tom would approve. A girl needs a man now and then.'

Helga, suddenly close to tears, turned away.

'Yes ... a girl needs a man.'

'There it is, dear.' Mrs. Joyce's voice sank a tone. 'That's life, isn't it?' She picked up the coffee tray. 'You have a lovely morning. I'll get on. Tom always said I talk too much,' and she bustled into the kitchen.

A lovely morning?

Helga stared out at the sun-soaked beach. What was she going to do? Swim alone? Go to the Ocean Beach club and listen to the yak of those ghastly women in their dreadful flowered hats and to the raddled, fat men who would stare at her, wondering and speculating?

She remembered Herman, and with an effort she called the hospital. The receptioness told her gently that there was no change.

Mrs. Joyce came from the kitchen.

'Is the poor dear still bad?' she asked.

'Yes.' Helga got to her feet. 'I'll take a swim.'

'You do that, dear. I had to give up swimming after my miscarriage, but sea water is good for you.'

Helga flinched.

When a middle aged woman gets hot pants for a boy young enough to be her son, cold water helps.

She went upstairs, put on a bikini, then walked across the stretch of sand and into the sea. She floated in the blue, warm water, staring up at the sky, looking at the nodding heads of the palm trees, hearing the murmur of motorboats and the distant roar of the traffic.

A paradise, she thought, if only she had someone with whom to share it.

A girl needs a man.

If only Herman would die! As she floated in the warm sea his death seemed to be the only solution. Once free of him, with sixty million dollars, she would be able to make a new life for herself with some virile, attentive man to take care of her.

A new life!

But she had an instinctive feeling that Herman wouldn't die for years. He would slowly recover. He would regain his speech. He would tell Winborn to cut her out of his will.

Utterly depressed, she swam back to the beach. Half an hour later, leaving Mrs. Joyce busy with the vacuum cleaner, she drove in the Mini to the Ocean Beach club. The secretary, beaming, was there to welcome her. She told him she was in the mood for a game of tennis. Could the pro give her a game? She was an expert player and the pro, over-weight, playing for years with the fat and the elderly, didn't realize what had hit him when Helga, her mood vicious, gave him the game of his life. She finally beat him 9–7. 6–1. 6–0.

'You are a splendid player, Mrs. Rolfe,' he gasped, towelling himself. 'The best game I've had since I played Riggs.'

Men!

She smiled at him. 'I was in the mood.'

Leaving him to chew on his defeat, she got in the Mini and drove to a small sea-food restaurant. She picked at a tough lobster in a white wine sauce. While she sat alone in the shade of the palm trees watching the young, the middle aged and the old on the beach, she thought of Dick.

If he hadn't broken his arm, she thought, he just might have come and just might have lain beside her on the king's size bed.

All this stupid talk about Voodoo! This was something she just wouldn't accept! How could a man like Gritten talk such nonsense!

Her mind shifted to Terry Shields. What was she doing? Then she thought of Jackson. Impatiently, she signalled to the waiter for her cheque.

The time now was 14.20. She had the whole afternoon, the evening and the night to face alone. *A girl needs a man.* How true! And yet, how dangerous! Again she thought of Herman with his twisted mouth forming the word whore. Patience, she told herself. You could be lucky. He could die. Then the magic key would be hers!

Getting into the Mini, she drove back to the villa. Mrs. Joyce was preparing to leave.

'There you are, ducks,' she said. 'Did you have a lovely morning?'

'Yes, thank you.' Helga forced a smile. 'And you?'

'Yes ... I like cleaning. It's my life, ducks. Tom always said I was a two-legged vacuum cleaner.' She laughed. 'Men! They don't even think of dust.' She closed one eye. 'We know what they think of, don't we, Mrs. Rolfe?'

I know what I think of too, Helga thought.

'Yes. You're right.'

'The boy came and fixed your bedroom shutter, dear,' Mrs. Joyce said. 'I'll be in again at seven. I'll bring you a nice slice of fish or is there anything else you fancy?'

'No, fish will be fine.'

Helga watched the big woman ride away on her bicycle,

then she walked into the living room. She looked around. The emptiness of this luxurious room and its silence weighed down on her. She went upstairs and took a shower, then going to the closet, she reached for her white pyjama suit. Taking it off the hanger, she paused to stare at it.

The pocket on the jacket, bearing her initials, had been neatly cut away.

For a long moment she stood staring at the jacket, puzzled. Then for no reason she could explain, she felt a creepy sensation run over her. She dropped the jacket as if it had become some horrible insect. She looked around the room, her heart racing. What did this mean? Who had done this? Mrs. Joyce? Unthinkable!

The boy came and fixed your bedroom shutter.

She crossed the room and examined the two wooden shutters. They were locked into place. She hadn't bothered to use them the previous night. She unlocked them and swung them to and fro. They worked perfectly. Re-locking them, she turned and looked around the bedroom. Her eyes went to the white jacket lying on the floor. She hesitated, then picked it up. She examined the neatly cut stitches. Someone had used a razor blade to remove the pocket. But why? With a little grimace she took the jacket into the bathroom and dropped it into the laundry basket.

She looked at her watch. God! How time crawled! It was 14.50. She went to the closet and examined all her clothes. None had been tampered with. She was aware how fast her heart was beating and she was angry with herself. There must be some reason for whoever it had been to cut off the pocket. This workman who had come to fix the shutter? She had read of perverted men who stole women's pants from laundry lines. Was this workman like that? She was sure Mrs. Joyce wouldn't have done it.

She drew in a deep breath, trying to calm herself.

She would talk to Mrs. Joyce this evening. She felt an odd atmosphere in the villa – a strange feeling – that bothered her. She felt she couldn't stay here for the rest of the afternoon. She must get out ... do something, but what?

She put on a yellow linen dress, selected shoes and a handbag, then went down to the living room. She walked out on to the terrace and looked at her own private beach: a quarter of a mile of lonely, deserted sand and sea and she turned away.

She couldn't stay here on her own. The Ocean Beach club? Very soon it would be time for tea. She thought of those old freaks eyeing the cake trolley. Goddamn it! she thought to herself, even *they* are better than this loneliness.

She locked up, then getting into the Mini, she drove to the club. For the next two hours, she sat listening to the local gossip, watched old fat fingers pointing to cakes as the waiter served, drank two cups of tea, aware the men were preening themselves as they gathered around her. She was asked to make up a fourth at bridge and, as she still had time to kill, she accepted. Her partner, a retired General, was delighted to have her on his side. The other two: a thin, sour faced old lady and her husband who was plump and boisterous, played well, but Helga, as with everything she took up, was in the professional class. Her devastating memory and her ruthless bids completely pulverized her opponents who she later learned were regarded as the club's best players.

She quickly became bored with this feeble opposition and at the end of the second game she excused herself saying she had an urgent appointment. The General who had scarcely contributed to the score was wreathed with smiles while the other two immediately began a fierce post-mortem.

Helga returned to the villa at 18.50. She was mixing herself a vodka-martini when she heard Mrs. Joyce arrive.

As the big woman bustled into the kitchen, carrying a shopping bag, Helga said, 'Join me in a drink, Mrs. Joyce.'

'Not for me, ducks. If I smell a cork, I get tiddly. My Tom never touched a drop.' She put the shopping basket down. 'I've got you a lovely fillet of kingfish. I miss the English fish, like turbot, but this is really nice. Have it grilled, dear, with peas and rice. You'll enjoy it.'

'It sounds wonderful. I wish I could cook. May I watch you, Mrs. Joyce?'

'I'm sure you do many things, dear. Cooking isn't difficult. So many women make a commotion about it. I say, if you like eating, cooking is a pleasure.'

Resting her hips against the kitchen table, Helga lit a cigarette. She watched Mrs. Joyce prepare the fish.

'About my bedroom shutter, Mrs. Joyce. Who was this workman?'

Having washed the fish fillet, Mrs. Joyce wiped her hands.

'Who was he, dear?' She looked sharply at Helga. 'He told me you had asked him to come.'

'It must have been the estate agent, Mr. Mason. I didn't know the shutter was out of order.'

'The boy said it needed oiling.' Mrs. Joyce put a saucepan of water on to boil. 'He was a nicely mannered boy. I felt sorry for him with his arm in plaster.'

Helga slopped her drink. Somehow she kept her face expressionless.

Dick!

'Did you leave him alone at all, Mrs. Joyce?'

The big woman stared at Helga.

'Did he steal something?'

'No, but did you leave him alone in my bedroom?'

'He came at the wrong moment, dear. I was cleaning the bath. I left him alone for no more than a couple of minutes. Is there something wrong?'

'I found some of my clothes disturbed.'

'Your clothes? A boy like that wouldn't touch your clothes.'

'No. Well, it doesn't matter.'

'There is something wrong, isn't there?' Mrs. Joyce looked distressed. 'If he took anything, I'd tell the police, dear. The police here are ever so helpful.'

'He didn't take anything.' Helga looked at her watch. 'It's all right. I'll catch the news.'

'News!' Mrs. Joyce snorted. 'You can do without the news, ducks. You turn on the telly and all you get is misery.'

Helga walked into the living room.

So Dick had been here. Dick had taken the pocket of her pyjama suit. Why?

She remembered what Gritten had said: *I can assure you that Jones is just as dangerous as Mala Mu was. The police suspect that Jones learned a lot from Mala Mu and he is now practising witchcraft.*

Utter rubbish, she told herself, and yet, there was this creepy atmosphere in the villa.

She forced herself to listen to the news: hi-jacking, two murders, industrial strife and five hostages held to ransom.

How right Mrs. Joyce was: all you get is misery.

Mrs. Joyce came in and began to set the table.

'Just ready, ducks,' she said. 'Sit you down.'

Still thinking of Dick, Helga moved to the table and sat down. She was surprised and pleased to see a half-bottle of Chablis waiting.

Mrs. Joyce served the meal.

'I thought you'd like a glass of wine, dear,' she said. 'You pour it. I'm not good at that kind of thing.'

'You are very thoughtful, Mrs. Joyce.'

'I know a lady of quality when I see one, dear. Now go ahead and tuck in.'

'This looks delicious.'

'I'm sure you will like it. Now tomorrow, I thought you might like to try the conch chowder. Being a fisherman's wife, I specialize in sea food and without making myself a liar, my conch chowder is the best on the island.'

'I would love that.' Helga found the kingfish excellent. Seeing Mrs. Joyce was prepared to gossip, she said, 'I spent the afternoon at the Ocean Beach club.'

'You did? Well I never! That surprises me, dear. That club is only fit for old fuddy-duddies ... not for a girl like you.'

Helga warmed to this woman.

'While I am waiting for Mr. Rolfe to recover, I have to do something.'

'You're right. Waiting is always bad. What a pity there isn't some nice man to take you around. Nassau is full of interest.'

'At the club, we got talking. Do you believe in Voodoo?' Helga looked sharply at Mrs. Joyce who abruptly lost her happy expression.

'Voodoo? You've been talking about that evil thing?'

'There were a couple of old people who seem to think it exists. What do you think?'

'Mrs. Rolfe ...' The big woman was suddenly serious. 'I

am, I hope, a good christian. I don't believe in meddling with what the black people do. You ask if Voodoo exists. It does. A lot of nasty things go on in the native quarter. My Tom told me to have nothing to do with it and he knew.'

'Nasty things? What kind of things, Mrs. Joyce?'

'Magic . . . some of the black people make magic.'

Helga ate for a moment, then asked, 'Magic? What sort of magic?'

'Mrs. Rolfe there are things best not talked about. You eat up your dinner and don't let it get cold.'

'But it interests me. Please tell me.'

Mrs. Joyce hesitated, then leaning her bulk against the kitchen doorway, she said, 'Well, dear, these black people can do things. I don't listen to the tales that go on here, but I do know there was a little boy living next door to me. His father was a fisherman like my Tom. One day a black man came and asked him for money. The fisherman hit him and threw him out. A day later, the little boy fell ill and went into a coma. The doctors could do nothing for him. Then finally the fisherman went to see this black man and gave him all his savings and the little boy recovered the next day. I saw all this with my own eyes. There are so many other tales. There was a dog who barked and barked and a neighbour just couldn't stand it. He went to the black man and paid him money. The next day the dog stopped barking and never barked again. I could go on and on, Mrs. Rolfe, but you finish your supper. I'll wash up.'

Mrs. Joyce went into the kitchen. Helga finished the fish, drank some of the wine, then lit a cigarette. She was frowning, her mind busy.

This is ridiculous, she told herself. Witchcraft! Magic! No, she would not accept this old wives' tale. Mrs. Joyce was as bad as Gritten. They had lived too long in the sun.

Mrs. Joyce reappeared and began clearing the table.

'Did you like it, dear? I've got coffee ready. Would you like it on the terrace?'

'That would be nice. The fish was wonderful.'

Helga went out on to the terrace and sat down. After a few minutes, Mrs. Joyce brought the coffee tray.

'There's a lovely Western on the telly, dear. Nothing like a

137

good Western,' she said as she poured the coffee. 'If you'll be all right, I'll get off.'

'Yes, of course. Then I'll see you tomorrow, and thank you for everything.'

'I'll be in at eight. Have a nice evening, dear.'

'And you too.'

It was only when Helga watched Mrs. Joyce ride away that she realized how lonely and empty this villa was. Impatiently, she got up and turned on the submerged lights in the pool. She wasn't in the mood to watch television. Sitting down again, she drank the coffee. She was now beginning to wish she had remained at the Diamond Beach hotel. At least there would be people in the lounge to watch. If it hadn't been for Dick she would have Hinkle to keep her company.

She stared at the moonlit beach. The silence, except for the gentle murmur of the sea, was oppressive. Could she spend the next three hours like this, staring at the empty sea, before going to bed? It was so lonely. She felt completely cut off. She could, of course, drive to the club and play more bridge, but that would be even worse than sitting here on her own.

While at the club that afternoon she had bought three paperbacks. She decided to settle here and read.

She went into the living room and looked at the books she had bought. Deciding on a historical novel (even greater than 'Gone With The Wind') she started back to the terrace, then paused.

She had a sudden instinctive feeling that she was being watched. She stood motionless in the middle of the big room, listening. Only the sound of the sea came to her. Then the thud of a falling coconut.

Again she experienced the creepy feeling she had already experienced when she had found the pocket of her pyjama suit had been removed. She had always prided herself on her strong nerves, but it came to her with an unpleasant impact that if an intruder arrived, apart from the telephone, she was completely unprotected.

But who would come here? she thought, irritated with her sudden uneasiness. She was imagining things!

Bracing herself, aware her heart was beating too quickly,

she walked out on to the terrace. The soft light from the swimming pool seemed to her now to produce an eerie effect. Even the moon now seemed to cast a sinister light.

She paused still conscious that she was not alone ... that someone was watching her.

But who?

Some black man? He could sneak up on her. Her screams would be lost in this lonely place.

Forcing steel into her voice, she called out, 'Is someone here?'

There was a long pause while she stood there, now frightened, then she heard a rustle from a big clump of shrubs close by and her heart skipped a beat.

'Who is it?'

'It is all right, Mrs. Rolfe ... it's only me.'

Out of the darkness, into the dim light, the figure of a man appeared.

Helga caught her breath sharply.

'It's me ... Harry Jackson.'

She stared for a long moment at the shadowy figure, then her alarm turned to fury.

'How dare you come here! You will leave at once or I will call the police!'

Jackson moved further into the light. She saw he was carrying a small cardboard box and he was wearing his best suit.

'I'm sorry, Mrs. Rolfe.' His voice was husky. 'I need your help and you need my help. I didn't mean to startle you.'

'You heard what I said! Leave at once or I'll call the police!'

He moved to the terrace table and put down the cardboard box.

'Please look at this, Mrs. Rolfe.'

He took off the lid and pushed the open box towards her.

Her heart hammering, Helga stared down at the small wooden doll lying in the box: a male doll with a balding head, miniature dark glasses, dressed in white silk pyjamas.

The likeness to Herman was so shocking, she only just suppressed a scream.

Embedded in the doll's head was a long, glittering needle.

A small black cloud drifted across the face of the moon. A sudden breeze rustled the palm trees.

Jackson said in a quavering voice, 'I can't stand it any longer. I've got to leave here. Only you can help me.'

'What is this?' She pointed to the doll.

He dropped into a chair and hiding his face in his hands, he began to cry: the snivelling noise a small boy makes when he has hurt himself.

Helga stared at him, then at the obscene doll. She realized she had nothing to fear from Jackson. He was a weak, slobbering male-less thing worthy only of contempt, but the doll scared her.

For a moment she stood thinking, aware she was feeling cold. Then she went quickly into the living room, to the cocktail cabinet and poured two stiff brandies. She carried the glasses back to the terrace.

'Drink this and stop snivelling!' The snap in her voice reacted on Jackson who grabbed the glass and drained it.

'I must have money, Mrs. Rolfe! I must get away from here! I have information to sell.'

'You have?' She was now in command of herself. She sat down and lit a cigarette. 'You're getting nothing from me, but you will explain about this doll or I will call the police!'

'I have information to sell,' Jackson whined. 'I swear you will get value for money, Mrs. Rolfe. I've got to leave here! That little half-caste bastard is going to get me killed!'

Helga forced herself to look again at the doll. It was unmistakably an effigy of Herman Rolfe. Around the doll's neck hung a tiny plastic bag which had something in it.

'Who made this?'

'He did ... Jones. He said he could stop you leaving Nassau by putting Mr. Rolfe into a coma! He said that by putting a needle in the doll's head Mr. Rolfe would go into the coma!'

Helga felt a shiver run through her. She remembered what Mrs. Joyce had said about the little boy living next door to her. She also recalled the puzzled, worried expressions on the faces of Dr. Bernstein, Dr. Levi and Dr. Bellamy. Was this possible? Could a needle driven into the head of a doll have sent Herman into this mysterious coma? She remembered what Gritten had said: *when I first came here, I thought like you that Voodoo was nonsense. I also didn't believe a man could walk on the moon.*

Stop this stupid thinking! she told herself. You know such things can't happen! There is a joker in the pack somewhere! This snivelling man is trying to con you!

'You had better explain,' she said, her voice unsteady.

'That's why I am here.' Jackson clenched and unclenched his hands. 'I need money, Mrs. Rolfe. Give me five thousand and I'll tell you everything.'

She regarded him contemptuously.

'If you persist in trying to blackmail me, I'll call the police and you can explain everything to them!'

He cringed.

'You wouldn't want the police to know about this, Mrs. Rolfe. I'm not trying to blackmail you. I swear I'm not! I must have money to leave here. The information I can give you is worth much more than five thousand. Jones is carving a doll to resemble you. He stole a bit of silk with your initials on it to make the doll's dress. He said he must have something belonging to the person he wants to control.' With a shaking finger, Jackson pointed to the tiny plastic bag hanging around the doll's neck. 'In that bag, Mrs. Rolfe, are nail parings belonging to your husband. Jones got them when he cleaned the hotel suite. I'm telling you, Mrs. Rolfe, he is planning to kill you.'

Although shaken, Helga stubbornly refused to accept this.

'I've told you, Jackson! Get out! I've had enough of this nonsense!'

'Jones has bled me white! I've got no money!' Jackson wailed. 'I've got to get off this island! Lopez is already hunting for me! Mrs. Rolfe, for God's sake, give me some money! If Jones hadn't broken his arm he would have finished the doll and by now you would be dead!'

Staring at his frightened, sweating face, Helga suddenly became frightened. *By now you would be dead.* She recalled Gritten's serious face. She recalled Mrs. Joyce's change of expression when she had asked about Voodoo. Was this possible?

With an effort, she forced herself to say, 'I have had enough of this nonsense. Get out!'

Jackson stared hopelessly at her, then lifted his hands in despair.

'Then I'll have to trust you to help me, Mrs. Rolfe. That girl ... Terry Shields.' He leaned forward. 'I can tell you who she is.'

'For the last time ... get out!'

'Jones and she are planning to get rid of you by Voodoo so she can inherit Rolfe's money!' Then stabbing his finger at her, Jackson went on, 'Terry Shields is your step-daughter! She is Sheila Rolfe who will inherit all her father's money if you are dead!'

CHAPTER EIGHT

HELGA reached for her glass of brandy while she struggled to absorb the shock of what Jackson had said. She forced herself to sip the brandy, knowing that Jackson was watching her for a reaction.

Terry Shields? Herman's daughter?

She thought of the girl with the Venetian red hair, the strong face, the wide, firm mouth and the big eyes. From the moment she had seen her, Helga had registered that this girl had character, that she was unusual, but Herman's daughter?

Then she remembered the cable to Hinkle: the cold, callous message:

Impossible to come to Nassau. Daddy will survive. He always does.

Did this stupid amateur blackmailer really think she would believe such a clumsy lie?

'Oh, get out! Mr. Rolfe's daughter is in Paris! I have proof of that!'

'That cable she sent to Hinkle?' Jackson shook his head. 'That was just a blind. She didn't want you to know she was here. She got a friend in Paris to send it. I heard her and Jones talking about it. I tell you, Mrs. Rolfe, Terry Shields is your step-daughter and she is planning to get rid of you.'

Helga hesitated. She couldn't bring herself to believe this but, looking at Jackson, she found it hard to believe he was lying and, besides, how did he know about the cable?

'I can check if you are lying,' she said, 'and if you are, I'll turn you over to the police. I mean this! Do you still say Terry Shields is Sheila Rolfe?'

He nodded.

'I swear it, but wait a moment, Mrs. Rolfe. If you are

143

satisfied I'm not lying, will you give me five thousand dollars to get away from here?'

'If you are not lying,' Helga said coldly, 'I will give you five hundred dollars which is enough for you to leave here.'

'Christ!' Jackson beat his fist together. 'You with all your money! I've got to get away! I've got to make a new start! What's five thousand to you?'

She got to her feet. 'Wait here.'

She went into the living room and called the Paradise City villa. The connection took a few minutes, then Hinkle's fruity voice came over the line.

'This is Mr. Herman Rolfe's residence.'

'Hinkle!' How glad and relieved she was to hear his voice! 'This is Mrs. Rolfe.'

'Ah, madame. I was about to take the liberty of telephoning you as I have not heard from you,' Hinkle said, reproach in his voice. 'I have just called the hospital. It appears there is no change.'

'No, I'm afraid not.' She paused, then went on, 'I'm sorry not to have called before, but I have been busy.'

'I am glad to hear that, madame. It must be lonely for you.'

Helga thought: Lonely? Could you or anyone else know how lonely?

'How is everything at the villa, Hinkle?'

'Not entirely satisfactory, madame. I am glad to be back, but I can assure you that by the time Mr. Rolfe and you return everything will be in order.'

'I am sure it will.' A pause, then she said, 'Did you get the cable I forwarded to you from Miss Sheila?'

'I did, madame. It distressed me.'

'Yes, but the young don't really care, do they? I am sure she is very busy.'

'It would appear so, madame.' Hinkle's voice sounded mournful.

'I have been thinking about Miss Sheila. I am disappointed not to have met her. When I think of a person it is helpful to have an image of them. Can you give me a description of her?'

144

'A description of her, madame?' Hinkle's voice went up a note.

'What is she like?' Helga held on to her patience.

'Well, madame, I would say she was a person of strong character.' Obviously, from his voice, Hinkle didn't approve of this conversation.

'But her appearance, Hinkle? Is she fat, thin, tall, short?'

'Miss Sheila has an excellent figure, madame. Like most young people she has improved on her appearance. She now has what I believe is referred to as Venetian red hair. It suits her very well.'

Helga experienced a little jolt. 'That is interesting.' She paused, then deliberately changing the subject, she went on, 'Have you any plans yet about Mr. Rolfe's study?'

'Indeed yes, madame. I have already consulted an interior decorator. I am sure, when Mr. Rolfe returns, he will be most satisfied.'

'Wonderful. All right, Hinkle. I am now going to play bridge. I just wanted to hear your voice.'

'You are most kind, madame.'

'And to say I miss your marvellous omelettes.'

As an exit line, she knew she couldn't have done better. She replaced the receiver.

So Jackson wasn't lying. This girl, calling herself Terry Shields, must be Herman's daughter!

Jones and she are planning to get rid of you by Voodoo so she can inherit Rolfe's money!

Could anything be more ridiculous? Then she thought of the doll with the needle in its head. She thought of Herman's mysterious coma. For a brief moment she felt frightened, then the steel in her asserted itself. *Know your enemy.* She could hear her father's dry, hard voice.

Now to handle Jackson. She would need to know everything he could tell her even if it cost her money.

She walked out on to the terrace. Jackson was sitting, slumped in his chair, a cigarette burning between his fingers. The reflected light from the swimming pool showed his face was shiny with sweat.

'Right, Jackson,' she said as she sat down. 'So this girl is

Sheila Rolfe. Now you start talking. I want to hear all about this. How did you find out who she was ... did she tell you?'

'Look, Mrs. Rolfe, if I don't have another drink, I'll flip my lid!'

'Help yourself. The drinks are in the living room,' Helga said impatiently. 'You don't expect me to wait on you, do you?'

He scrambled to his feet, and after a moment or so, returned with a bottle of brandy. He poured a drink, swallowed it, then poured more brandy into his glass.

'Now start talking, Jackson!'

'How about the money?' He leaned forward and peered at her. 'I'm not telling you anything more unless you promise to give me five thousand dollars!'

She could see he was slightly drunk and this made her uneasy. If he turned vicious there was nothing she could do about it. She must be careful how she handled him, she told herself.

'If what you have to tell me is worth so much, I will pay you.'

He grinned uneasily at her.

'It'll be worth it. Let's see the money, then I'll start talking.'

She thought of the eight thousand dollars upstairs in her bedroom. He mustn't know about that. He could over-power her, take the money and run.

'You don't imagine I keep a sum like that here? I will give you a cheque.'

He sipped more brandy, then shook his head.

'No cheques. I want cash.'

'That can be arranged. The Diamond Beach hotel will give me the money.'

He thought about this, then nodded.

'Yeah. Well, okay. Then it is agreed: I talk, I get five thousand ... right?'

She mustn't let him think he was beginning to intimidate her.

'Talk first, Jackson. It is for me to decide.'

He studied her, sipped more brandy, then set down his glass, his hand unsteady.

'You're a real toughie, aren't you?'

'Come on, Jackson ... how did you find out this girl is Sheila Rolfe?'

'She arrived on the same plane as you did,' Jackson said, sitting back in his chair. 'Acting on Rolfe's instructions I was at the airport to see you arrive. When you left, Sheila came up to me and asked me if I knew of a cheap pad.' He grinned. 'I attract the chicks, Mrs. Rolfe. They are always coming up and asking me dopey questions. Then she asked if you were Mrs. Herman Rolfe. I asked myself why this chick was interested in you so I got friendly with her. I drove her to a motel. I told her what my job was and that I was watching you. Then she said you were her step-mother so I asked her what she was doing here.' He blew out his cheeks. 'By this time, Mrs. Rolfe, she and I were very friendly. I get very friendly with chicks pretty fast.' He leered at her. 'You know that, don't you? I got very friendly with you, didn't I?'

'What did she say she was doing here?' Helga asked, her face like stone.

'She had seen in the papers her father had come here. She had always wanted to see Nassau. She had saved some money so she took off. Simple as that.'

'Did she see her father?'

'From a distance.' Jackson shrugged. 'From what she told me they don't hit it off.'

'And Jones. Where does he come in?'

'That little creep? Like I told you, he worked for me. If there's a snake ... it's Jones. I offered him a hundred dollars to search your apartment. When he found and read that letter to Winborn, the little bastard held me up for four thousand bucks to buy his goddamn motorbike. Then you blackmailed me and got the letter back. Then you started real trouble by telling him you wanted him in Paradise City. He came crying to me, but there was nothing I could do about it and I told him so. I won't forget the way he looked at me ... like a goddamn cornered rat. "I'm not going," he said. "I've got a way to stop her leaving here." He often used my beach hut to keep a lot of junk he didn't want his mother to know about. After I had shut up my office, I went out there and found him making this doll. He's damn clever with his hands. I asked him what he was doing and he said he was stopping you taking him to Paradise City. He said it was Voodoo magic. I told him he was crazy. I sat there watching him. When he had finished the doll, he drove the needle into the doll's head, then he began to bang on a drum. After a while, he said Rolfe was now too ill to travel. I again told him he was crazy. He gave me a sly little grin and told me to wait and see.'

Helga stared at the doll.

'This is utter rubbish and you know it!' she said angrily.

'Is it? What do you or I know about these coloured finks who live here? It worked, didn't it? You didn't take the fink to Paradise City, did you?'

'It just happened my husband became worse.'

Jackson shrugged.

'I'm telling you what happened. Now I'll tell you something else. Sheila came to my beach hut when I wasn't there and she met Jones. They hit it off. Don't ask me how he found out who she was, but he did. Maybe she told him. She liked boasting about her rich father. Now this fink is no dope. I told you he wanted to hold you up for five hundred thousand but you didn't believe me. He had read the letter and he knew Sheila was coming in for a million. He also knew just how rich Rolfe is. He thought why bother with a million? Why not grab the lot? With Rolfe and you out of the way, Sheila would get a lot more than a million. She and he were already rolling in the hay. So suppose he could persuade her to marry him? That's the way the fink began to plan, so first things first . . . he begins carving a doll like this.'

'Did Sheila know about this?'

'Maybe . . . maybe not. I don't know.' Jackson's eyes shifted from her direct stare.

'But he told you?'

'Yeah. When he bust his arm he couldn't get the doll finished so he came to me and offered to cut me in. He wanted me to get something of yours you had worn, but I wouldn't do it. So he did it himself, then the little bastard got scared I would talk so he called up Lopez and told him I was having it off with Maria.' Jackson wiped his sweating face

148

with the back of his hand. 'So Lopez is looking for me and I've got to get off the island pronto and I need money. This is where we came in, Mrs. Rolfe.'

'If you imagine I believe for one moment any of this, you need your head examined,' Helga said quietly. 'But to be rid of you, I will give you a thousand dollars and that is all.' She got to her feet. 'I'll get my bag.'

'Wait, baby.' Jackson leaned forward. 'I want more than that. You say Voodoo is rubbish. Want to gamble on it?' He pointed to the doll. 'Take that needle out of the head. See what happens. The fink said to get Rolfe out of his coma, he had only to remove the needle. Go ahead and do it! Then call the hospital.'

'Oh, stop it!' Helga snapped. 'I'm not listening to any more of this damn nonsense. I'll give you the money and you'll go!'

Jackson studied her.

'Wait, baby, don't rush this,' he said. 'I've got something very special to tell you. I read that letter to Winborn. I know if Rolfe lives you are out in the cold, but if he dies, you'll have no problems. You want the old ruin to die, don't you? You've been sitting around, willing him to die, haven't you? Okay, suppose you make an experiment? The fink told me – and baby, listen hard to this – that if he took the needle out of the doll's head and stuck it where the doll's heart is, Rolfe would be dead in minutes. That's how the fink was planning to get rid of you, once he had finished the other doll. Maybe you haven't the guts to do it, but for five thousand dollars, I'll do it. What do you say? You don't believe in Voodoo. Okay, I don't believe in it either, so let's see what happens. You promise me five thousand if Rolfe dies and I'll move the needle!'

Suppose it worked? The thought flashed into Helga's mind. Just suppose this ridiculous Voodoo theory wasn't ridiculous. Suppose this half-drunk amateur blackmailer by moving the needle killed Herman? The very idea was sheer fantasy but she remembered Gritten saying that twenty years ago who would imagine men walking on the moon? So suppose it worked?

It would mean she would be free, that she would control

an enormous sum of money and she wouldn't have to face the life of a nun!

She stared at the doll. It brought back the picture of Herman lying in bed, his useless arm propped on a pillow, saliva dripping from his slack mouth.

Suppose he did die? Wouldn't it be a blessing to him?

A sudden chill ran through her. No! This was a con trick! So far the cards had been falling her way, but now ... the joker in the pack!

Aware her heart was beating furiously, she said, 'I have had enough of this. I will give you a thousand dollars and no more. I have the money here. That is all you are going to get.'

'No, it isn't, baby. You know you want me to do it, but you haven't the guts to say so.' He reached out and took the doll from the box. 'You don't believe ... I don't believe.' He took hold of the needle and jerked it from the doll's head. 'Now, baby, five thousand and I'll fix this rich old bastard.'

Helga stepped back, knocking over her chair.

'No! Leave it alone!' Her voice was shrill.

Jackson grinned drunkenly at her.

'Let's experiment. You don't believe nor do I. So why not? Here we go!' Holding the needle, he pushed it slowly and steadily into the doll's chest. 'Now ... let's see what happens.'

She stood staring at the doll lying, impaled, on the table. Had she imagined that the doll had given a little jerk as the needle had entered?

'It's done, baby,' Jackson said. 'Give it ten minutes to work, then call the hospital. Who knows? You could be worth millions?'

A sudden dreadful panic seized hold of Helga. A terrifying and horrible atmosphere seemed to her to have come into the room like a poisonous, invisible cloud. She turned and ran blindly from the room and up the stairs and into her bedroom. She slammed and locked the door. As she looked wildly around the room, she heard Jackson come pounding up the stairs. She darted to the telephone, and after two attempts, managed to dial the operator.

Jackson hammered on the door.

'Open up, you stupid bitch!' he shouted. 'Don't use the phone!'

She listened to the burr-burr on the line as Jackson stood away from the door, braced himself against the wall, then lifting his leg, he drove his foot hard against the door lock. The door flew open and he stormed into the room.

Helga heard a voice say, 'Operator. What number do you want?'

As Helga screamed wildly, 'Police!' Jackson reached her, swung her away from the telephone and hit her on the side of her jaw with all the power of his panic-stricken arm. As she fell forward, he snatched up the telephone and slammed it down on her defenceless head.

Slowly, Helga drifted into consciousness. The first thing she became aware of was a curious weightlessness of her body. It was as if she was lying on a cloud. She was also aware of having no feeling in her limbs. She wondered if this was death. If it was, she thought, she would have no complaint. To float like this forever in a painless vacuum would be wonderful.

Then she became aware of distant voices: men's voices, hushed but continuous. Then one of the men cleared his throat noisily. She frowned. Did the dead clear their throats? She opened her eyes.

She saw that she was in the luxurious bedroom of the rented villa and she was lying in the king's size bed. She saw too that the sun was trying hard to penetrate the blinds, making white lines across the bed. She also saw the familiar figure of Nurse Fairely who was sitting by the window, peering out between the slots of the blind, and seeing her, Helga closed her eyes.

Then in spite of the feeling of weightlessness (she was probably under heavy sedation, she told herself), her mind became active. She remembered screaming for the police and seeing Jackson rushing at her. She remembered seeing his fist flying towards her and seeing a flash of white, searing light.

Lying in the comfortable bed, completely relaxed, she now realized her mistake in calling the police. How much better it would have been to have given Jackson all the money in the villa and to have got rid of him. Now, because she had panicked, here was a complete and utter mess. Had Jackson been caught? The telephone operator would have immediately alerted the police, but it would have taken at least ten minutes – probably longer – for a patrol car to have arrived. Had Jackson, who must have heard her scream for the police, got away in time?

If they caught him, the whole sordid story would come out. She recalled the gruesome commotion when Herman had had his stroke. The newspaper men like jackals, the T.V. cameras, the photographers! She could imagine the headlines: *Mrs. Herman Rolfe attacked in a lonely villa.* If Jackson were caught, he would tell how he had been hired by Herman to watch her because Herman no longer trusted her. (Imagine the sensation that would cause!) He would also tell about Herman's letter to Winborn (more and great sensation!) and then how she had been trying to force Dick to go to Paradise City (sensational hints of seduction). The police would pick up Dick and he would talk. He might even say she was trying to get him into her bed!

A mess! You play your cards, you take some tricks, it looks like a winning hand, then along comes the Joker.

She wondered what the time was. How long had she been unconscious? From the feel of the sun on the bed, she thought it could be early afternoon.

She opened her eyes and through her long lashes, she regarded Nurse Fairley who was now looking at a glossy magazine, her fat face in repose. Her peaceful expression revealed inner contentment. Watching her, Helga felt a pang of envy. This woman was engaged in good and satisfying work. She probably never had any nagging problems and certainly no compulsive sex urge.

Then Helga saw the door open and Dr. Levi came in. Nurse Fairely got heavily to her feet.

'How is she?' Dr. Levi whispered.

'Still sleeping, doctor.'

'Hello,' Helga said and was irritated her voice came as a whisper. 'So you have come to look after me.'

Levi came silently to the bed.

152

'Don't talk, Mrs. Rolfe.' His deferential voice annoyed her. 'Everything is all right. You are under sedation. Just sleep. There is nothing to worry about.'

Perhaps there were some spineless women who would welcome this smooth, bedside manner, but it infuriated Helga. What did he imagine she was? One of those self-pitying, soft-centred, must-have-a-tranquillizer women without guts?

'I will talk as much as I like,' she snapped and was delighted that her voice had come back and with it its steel. 'I'm not dying, am I?'

Startled Levi said, 'Of course not, but you have concussion and a very badly bruised jaw, Mrs. Rolfe. It is better for you to try to relax and sleep.'

'What happened to that man ... the man who attacked me?' she demanded. She had to know. 'Did the police get him?'

'Now please don't worry ...'

'Did they get him?' Her voice became shrill.

'Not yet, Mrs. Rolfe. Now do please calm yourself. You need rest.'

She drew in a breath of relief. Had Jackson had time to find her bag and take the money? She hoped so for it would mean he was off the island by now. She wanted him well out of the reach of the police.

'Yes.' She closed her eyes.

'I'll see you this evening, Mrs. Rolfe. The police are most anxious to question you, but I have told them you are not to be disturbed.'

Helga flinched. She hadn't thought that the police would ask probing questions.

'I don't want to see them just yet.'

'Certainly not. You have a nice, little sleep.'

She restrained herself from snapping at him. He was treating her like a moron!

She heard him whispering to Nurse Fairely, then the door closed. Lying still, Helga's mind became busy. What was she to tell the police? Suppose Jackson had got away? Could she lie herself out of this mess? She could tell the police it was some coloured man who had attacked her. She thought about this. As the police hadn't caught Jackson as he had left the villa, surely it meant they hadn't seen him. If she could keep Jackson out of this, then the whole sordid story could be swept under the rug.

She would have to be careful. A coloured man! This could be the solution! They would want a description. Her mind worked busily: tall, thin, middle-aged with a coloured handkerchief around his head, a dirty white shirt, dark trousers, bare feet. That description would match hundreds of the natives she had seen in the market and on the beach.

The more she thought about this, the safer it seemed. No one had seen Jackson arrive. It wasn't likely he would have told anyone he was coming to get money from her. The weakness was if the police had seen Jackson run off. She decided to play it off the cuff. She was confident she could dominate a police officer.

'Here is a nice cup of tea, Mrs. Rolfe,' Nurse Fairely said, breaking into her thoughts. 'I'm sure you must feel like a comforting drink.'

'I think I do.' She opened her eyes and managed a smile.

'And here is something to help you to sleep.'

Obediently she swallowed the small capsule, then with the nurse's help, she drank some of the tea.

Some minutes later, she drifted into a sleep that was empty of dreams, of fear, and of the coming problems she knew she would have to face.

When she awoke, she was conscious that her head was aching and her mouth sore, but she no longer felt dopey nor weightless. The sedation was over, she told herself with relief. From now on, her mind must be razor sharp. She looked around, then lifted her head from the pillow, wincing a little.

Nurse Fairely came to her.

'How do you feel, Mrs. Rolfe?'

'My head aches.' She touched the side of her face. It felt swollen and tender. 'What time is it?'

'Just after eight. You slept beautifully all night.'

She stared at the nurse.

'Is it another day? Have you been up all night?'

Nurse Fairely smiled.

154

'Oh no, we have a night nurse. Do you fancy some breakfast? A lightly boiled egg? Tea?'

'Tea, I think. Nothing to eat. My mouth's as sore as hell.'

'That's not to be wondered at.' Nurse Fairely moved to the door. 'I'll get you tea and I'll give you something for your headache.'

'No more pills,' Helga said firmly.

Nurse Fairely left the room and Helga made the effort to sit up. For a moment her head swam, then apart from the dull ache, she suddenly felt fine.

Then the door opened and Hinkle, carrying a tea tray, came in.

'Hinkle!' Helga exclaimed, delighted. 'Why, bless you! When did you arrive?'

'Yesterday afternoon, madame. As soon as I heard the distressing news.'

'Thank you, Hinkle. I only wish now I hadn't sent you away.'

'It was most unfortunate, madame.'

She looked sharply at him as he poured the tea. He looked more like a grieving father than a bishop this morning. Her heart warmed to him. I really believe he cares about me, she thought. He must be the only person in the world who does.

'Prop me up, Hinkle,' she said. 'I'm dying for a cup of tea.'

'I trust madame, you are not suffering too badly,' he said as he gently arranged her pillows, then handed her the tea.

'It's all right.' She sipped the tea, then went on, 'Tell me, Hinkle, what's going on? I suppose the press have arrived?'

'Indeed yes, madame. They are outside waiting for a statement. Mr. Winborn will be arriving this afternoon.'

'Winborn?' She frowned. 'What does he want for God's sake?'

'Dr. Levi thought he should be here to handle the press.'

She asked the vitally important question.

'Have they found the man who attacked me?'

'Apparently not, madame. The Inspector is anxious to see you. He wants a description of the man. Dr. Levi has told him he must wait.'

Helga felt a surge of triumph run through her.

'Didn't the police see him?'

'No, madame. They arrived too late.'

So once again the cards were falling her way! There would now no longer be a mess!

'I'll see the Inspector sometime this morning, Hinkle.'

'Yes, madame.'

Helga again looked sharply at him. She was surprised that he hadn't asked questions. How it happened? Who was the man? Then she saw there was a distressed, shocked expression on Hinkle's face, so distressed that she put down the cup of tea.

'Is there something wrong, Hinkle?'

He hesitated, then nodded.

'I am afraid so, madame. Dr. Levi suggested that I should break the news to you.'

An icy chill began to crawl up Helga's spine.

'News? What news?'

'It's Mr. Rolfe, madame. I very much regret to tell you he died the night before last. Apparently, madame, he came out of the coma for a few brief moments, then his heart gave out.'

Into Helga's mind came the scene of Jackson withdrawing the needle and then slowly pushing it into the doll's chest.

She was now so cold she began to shiver.

'I can't believe it,' she said hoarsely. 'What time the night before last?'

'It would be about the time you were attacked, madame. This will be a terrible shock to you as it is to me. I know how both of us, madame, will miss him.'

Helga stared at the kind, distressed face and she put her hands to her eyes.

'But you should think, madame, that it is really a happy release. He suffered so much and he was so very brave.' Then as she began to weep, Hinkle went silently from the room, stopping Nurse Fairely from entering.

'Madame would like a few moments to herself, nurse,' he said in a whisper. 'She has been so good, so worthy and so loyal to him. It is a most grievous loss to her.'

Listening to his words, Helga shuddered.

'So good, so worthy, so loyal!'

She again saw Herman's contorted face and his slack mouth forming the word whore.

Burying her face in the pillow, she began to sob her heart out.

The next four hours were the worst Helga had ever lived through for they were hours of self-incrimination, remorse and self-disgust. She saw herself as she imagined others saw her. It was like looking into a three dimensional mirror and what she saw there sickened her.

When Nurse Fairely had come in, hearing Helga sobbing, Helga had screamed at her to get out and stay out.

As soon as the startled nurse had withdrawn, Helga had staggered out of bed and had locked the door, then she had returned to the bed to continue her desperate sobbing.

An hour of this left her drained and leaving the bed, she put on a wrap and had sat in a lounging chair.

There came a gentle tap on the door and Hinkle's voice asking, 'May I bring something, madame? A little beef tea?'

'Just leave me alone.' Helga had to control herself not to scream at him. 'I'll ring if I want anything.'

Then began the long hours of self-incrimination. So Herman is dead, she thought. You wanted him to die. You longed for him to die because you wanted to own all his money. That was all you could think about . . . his money! Now finally he is dead and he died hating you. After the few years you have been married to him during which time he respected you, was proud of you, trusted you, he finally died hating you.

The knowledge that he had died hating her crushed her.

Because of her infernal sex urge she had been unfaithful, but she had always been scrupulously honest with his money and yet he had died believing she had not only been unfaithful but was no longer to be trusted with the handling of his fortune.

He had called her a whore. He had died thinking of her as a whore.

Her mind switched to what Hinkle had said: *Apparently, madame, he came out of the coma for a few moments, then his heart gave out.*

She saw Jackson pulling the needle out of the doll's head and pushing it into the doll's body. Could the needle have killed Herman? Hadn't she stood by, doing nothing, while Jackson had murdered her husband? Why hadn't she snatched the doll from him? Wasn't it because she longed for Herman to die, and although she didn't believe it could happen, had hoped it would happen?

Stop this stupid, superstitious thinking! she told herself. You know a needle couldn't kill anyone. It's not possible. Herman's death was a coincidence. It must have been! There could be no other explanation.

Her mind switched back to Herman's hatred. She thought of his letter to Winborn. Only a few days ago, she had told herself that when Herman died, she would destroy the letter.

Because he no longer trusted her, Herman had written this letter which would strip her of her V.I.P. status since she would never accept the conditions he laid down.

As I am satisfied that she has betrayed my trust ...

She remembered his words.

True, she thought, I did betray your trust but you never considered my feelings. All you wanted was a good looking secretary-servant. Although I was unfaithful to you I have always been honest with your money. Why couldn't you have shown a spark of kindness, consideration and understanding and have turned a blind eye to my affairs?

For many minutes, she sat still, staring out of the window, then she came to a decision.

You may be a selfish, hard, unfaithful bitch, but you are not dishonest, she told herself.

She would not destroy the letter. She would give it to Winborn when he arrived. Whatever else she was, she wasn't dishonest nor a cheat. To destroy the wishes of a dead man would be a despicable and utterly dishonest act.

Then into her mind came the small voice of temptation. Don't do anything in haste, the voice said. Think what you will be giving up. Think of the power that will be yours when you control sixty million dollars. If you give that letter to Winborn, knowing you can't live like a nun, you will have nothing and you will be faced with the task of making a new life for yourself. Think of the gossip when it becomes known that Herman has disinherited you. They will say gleefully that there is no smoke without fire. The Federal tax people will want to know what has happened to the two million dollars Archer stole. You will have to throw him to the wolves to save yourself and he will tell the world, to try to save himself, you were his mistress. Don't give the letter to Winborn, the small voice urged. Destroy it as you were planning to do before you got this spineless feeling of guilt. No one will know except Hinkle and he is your friend. He admires you: *so good, so worthy, so loyal.*

For more than three hours, Helga struggled with the small voice and then when she felt utterly exhausted, the steel in her asserted itself.

Whatever else you are, whatever else you become, she said, half aloud, you will not be a cheat!

Her mind made up, she got unsteadily to her feet, rang the service bell, then unlocked the door. She crossed to the wall mirror and regarded herself. God! She looked terrible! The right side of her face was puffy and bruised. Her eyes were swollen with weeping. Her hair looked like a bird's nest.

She crossed to the desk and sat down as a tap came on the door.

'Come in.'

Hinkle entered and closed the door gently.

'I want you to do something for me, Hinkle,' she said and taking out a sheet of notepaper, she wrote:

Please give Mr. Hinkle, the bearer of this note, the envelope you have in safe keeping for me.

She signed and addressed an envelope to the Manager of the Diamond Beach hotel.

'Will you please go immediately to the Diamond Beach hotel and bring back an envelope they are keeping for me in their safe?'

'Certainly, madame.' Hinkle took the note, hesitated, then said, 'May I inquire if you are still in pain, madame? Nurse Fairely is extremely worried.'

She looked at him, her eyes steely.

'I am all right. Will you tell the police inspector I will see him when it is convenient to him?'

'Are you sure that is wise, madame? Shouldn't you . . .'

'Please do as I say!'

'Yes, madame.' Hinkle flushed at her sharp tone. 'I have had a telephone call from Mr. Winborn. He will not be arriving this evening but sometime early tomorrow. It would seem there is an airport strike that has delayed him. He sends his regrets.'

'All right. Now please go to the hotel.'

When he left, looking upset by her curt manner, she went into the bathroom and began repairing her face. In twenty minutes she had painted out the bruise, reduced the swelling of her eyes and fixed her hair. She was lighting a cigarette when Chief Inspector Harrison arrived.

Harrison was a tall burly man who could have been Frank Gritten's brother. He had the same steely blue eyes and the same gentle voice.

He began by offering his sincere condolences but Helga cut him short.

'Thank you, Inspector. I am anxious to rest. I understand you want a description of the man who attacked me. He was coloured: tall, thin, middle aged and he wore a yellow and red handkerchief around his head, a dirty white shirt, dark trousers and was bare footed. Is there anything else you want to know?'

Startled at being so hustled, Harrison stared blankly at her.

'You haven't seen this man before, madame?'

'No.'

'Is there anything missing?'

Why hadn't she thought to look to see if Jackson had taken the money? Helga was angry with herself for not checking.

'I don't think so. This is a hired villa. I have only my jewels and some money ... nothing else of value.' She got to her feet and going to the closet, she checked her jewel box, then satisfied, she went to her bag lying on the dressing table. The eight thousand dollars was missing! With an effort, she kept her face expressionless. Snapping the bag shut, she said, 'No, there's nothing missing. It was fortunate I was up here. I heard movements, went to the head of the stairs and saw this man. He saw me and came bounding up the stairs. I locked myself in and I called the police. He broke in and tried to stop me telephoning. I suppose he became frightened and ran away.'

Harrison regarded her thoughtfully.

'It would seem so, madame.'

'Is that all?' she asked impatiently.

'Not quite all. What can you tell me about a doll we found downstairs?'

She had completely forgotten about the doll. Again her steel control served her well.

'Doll? I know nothing about a doll. What do you mean?' She crushed out her cigarette.

'Excuse me a moment.' Harrison went to the door. He spoke to someone outside, then returned, carrying Rolfe's effigy.

'This doll, madame.'

Helga forced herself to look at the doll.

'I've never seen it before.' She looked more closely, then shrank back, stifling a gasp, but she was careful not to overplay the scene. 'It – it resembles my husband.'

'Yes, madame. I am sorry to raise such a painful . . .'

'This intruder must have brought it with him. Probably, he wanted to sell it to me,' Helga said quickly. 'There can be no other explanation.'

'Unfortunately there is, madame. You may have heard of this Voodoo cult . . .'

'At this moment, I am not interested in cults,' Helga broke in, steel in her voice. 'If that is all, then I would be glad if you would go. My head is tormenting me.'

Harrison hesitated. He was very conscious that he was facing a woman now worth at least sixty million dollars and that kind of money drew a lot of water. He was also aware that she had just lost her husband and had been attacked. If he continued to question her she could complain and his superiors could come down on him like a ton of concrete. He decided to play safe.

'Certainly, madame. I will see you are not bothered again. As nothing has been stolen . . .' He began to move to the door. 'You can be sure we will hunt for this man.'

'I am sure you will,' Helga said and turned away.

When he had gone, she sat down and drew in a deep breath. That had gone off better than she could have hoped. So Jackson had found and taken the money. That must mean he was miles away by now. The mess she had feared was now disappearing under the rug. The cards had begun to fall her way again!

Twenty minutes later, Hinkle appeared with a large, sealed envelope.

'Is that what you wanted, madame?'

Helga slit open the envelope, glanced inside and saw the red folder.

'Yes, thank you, Hinkle.' She looked directly at him. 'I suppose you have guessed what this is?'

'I would rather not be told, madame,' Hinkle said, his face expressionless. 'I hesitate to offer advice, but may I suggest the contents of this envelope should be destroyed.'

She stared at him and again the small voice urged: go on, destroy it! Think what you have to lose! Even Hinkle is telling you to do it. Doesn't that salve your stupid conscience?

'Thank you, Hinkle. You are a good friend.'

'I suggest a light meal would be sensible, madame. One thinks so much better when fortified. Perhaps a dozen oysters?'

She shook her head.

'I feel like a big steak. I haven't eaten for two days!'

His face lit up.

'Certainly, madame. I will cook it myself. Also a little caviar with toast.'

As soon as he had gone, Helga decided to dress. Looking at her watch, she saw the time was 14.45. She hated slopping around in a wrap.

Half an hour later, when Hinkle pushed in the service trolley, she was wearing a white dress with a broad black leather belt around her slim waist and he regarded her with admiring approval.

'If I may say so, madame, you are a remarkable person.'

She smiled at him.

'Thank you, Hinkle. At times I believe that myself. You

162

didn't think ...' Then she stopped, seeing the cocktail shaker. 'Of course you did ... bless you.'

'I fear Dr. Levi wouldn't approve, madame, but in times of stress, a little alcohol is beneficial.'

After she had finished the meal and had drunk two vodka-martinis, she found to her surprise that her head no longer ached.

As she lit a cigarette, she asked, 'What are the ar-rangements?' She couldn't bring herself to say 'funeral', but Hinkle knew what she meant.

'I have attended to all that, madame. The service will be at the Church of Christ in Paradise City at three o'clock the day after tomorrow. Dr. Levi hopes you will be able to fly home in the executive plane tomorrow afternoon with Mr. Winborn.'

'It is not going to be a big affair?' she asked suddenly anxious.

'No, madame. Later, of course there will be a memorial service, but for the private service, just you, Mr. Winborn, the staff and Miss Sheila.'

Helga stiffened.

'Miss Sheila?'

'Yes, madame. She has arrived. I saw her this morning. She would like to meet you. If it would be convenient she would come here at six o'clock.'

Helga hesitated.

She thought of the red-headed girl and she could hear again those cruel words:

When a middle aged woman gets hot pants for a boy young enough to be her son, cold water helps.

Inwardly, she flinched.

Then she remembered the sacrifice she was going to make by giving Winborn the letter. Because she refused to cheat, this girl, now living rough, would suddenly become a millionairess! Surely this girl would admire her for her sacrifice and regret what she had said.

'Of course, Hinkle. I must see her.'

'Very well, madame.' Hinkle positively beamed. 'If you feel strong enough, it is quite safe for you to come downstairs and enjoy the sun. With the assistance of the police I have got rid of the press. The Inspector was good enough to leave a couple of men on guard to see you are not bothered. Dr. Levi will be coming in half an hour.'

'All right, Hinkle. I am so grateful for what you have done and are doing.'

With a happy expression on his fat face, Hinkle wheeled the trolley from the room.

Nervous and restless, Helga sat on the terrace under a sun umbrella. She kept looking at her watch. The time was 17.50. In ten more minutes the girl who called herself Terry Shields would arrive.

Dr. Levi had come and gone. He had offered tranquillizers, had warned her not to exert herself, had offered condolences and as Helga didn't encourage him, he finally bowed himself out.

Nurse Fairely also took her leave. Kind as she was, Helga was glad to see her go.

Now, she was alone except for Hinkle who she could hear pottering around in the kitchen, probably preparing something for dinner. She thought of Winborn. He would be arriving the following morning. Once he had read Herman's letter, his claws would be unsheathed, but she was beyond caring.

The sound of a discreet cough made her look around. Hinkle was standing in the doorway.

'Miss Sheila, madame,' he said and stood aside to let Terry pass around him, then he moved out of sight.

Helga watched the girl come across the patio with quick, purposeful strides. She was wearing a white T-shirt and dark blue jeans. Her red-gold hair glittered in the sun. She walked straight up to Helga and looked down at her.

'Are you all right?' she asked, and Helga was surprised at the concern in her voice.

'I've got over it, thank you. Won't you sit down?'

Terry pulled up a chair and sat down, her knees together, her slim hands in her lap.

'I owe you an apology and an explanation,' she said, looking directly at Helga. 'My exit line when we last met was

164

indefensible. All I can say is I regret saying it and hope you don't hate me for it. You see, Dick means a lot to me and when my men are threatened, I behave like an ill-mannered bitch.'

Taken aback, Helga said, 'You should never regret telling the truth. So Dick means a lot to you?'

'Yes. He intrigues me. I see a big future for him. I am re-educating him.'

'Are you? Will he appreciate that?'

'He needs to be re-educated. He realizes he is very mixed up. So many people are. I have explained that to him. It is not a matter of liking or appreciating. People don't like changes, but he accepts he must be re-educated. I intend to take him back to Paris with me. He will make a tremendous impact once he gets there.'

What the hell is all this? Helga asked herself, feeling bewildered.

'Impact?' she asked. 'In what way?'

'By his powers. He is a genuine Voodoo doctor.'

Helga stiffened.

'A Voodoo doctor? Surely you don't believe in that ridiculous cult?'

'It is only those who know absolutely nothing about Voodoo who talk like that,' Terry said quietly. 'There is good and evil Voodoo. Dick had an evil master. I'm going to teach him to do good with his powers.'

'I suppose you know he made an obscene effigy of your father?'

Terry nodded.

'Yes, but it wasn't obscene. He made it because you were forcing him to leave here. It was wrong, of course, but he was desperate and you mustn't forget he is young and very immature.'

'You really believe he put your father in a coma?'

'Of course.'

Helga suppressed a shudder.

'And you know he began to make a doll resembling me?'

'Yes, but I stopped that,' Terry said crisply. 'That is what I mean about evil Voodoo. I have got him over that now. In Paris he will have a large following. In time he may be like

165

the Guru with his Rolls Royce. People will flock to him once he has been re-educated.'

Helga felt bewildered. She shifted to more familiar ground.

'All this will cost money, won't it?'

Terry shrugged.

'Oh, money will come. Once Dick convinces people he is genuine, money will roll in.'

'But won't you need money to get him to Paris?'

'That's no problem. After I had talked to him, he sold his bike to some rich creep who couldn't wait six months for the next delivery. He got seven thousand dollars for it. No, money isn't important. The important thing is to keep him thinking on the right lines and to make sure he uses his powers in the right way.'

'You do realize he has done an evil thing and that he is also a thief?'

Terry smiled.

'But no longer.'

'Are you quite sure people will need a boy like Dick?'

'Of course, but why discuss it? I can see you don't understand. I suppose I am an odd ball but I like influencing people. I like putting ideas into their minds. Quite often those ideas grow rewardingly.'

Again Helga shifted ground.

'Why did you come to Nassau?'

Terry looked directly at her.

'I wanted a close-up of you. I was curious to see the woman my father married.'

'I can understand that. I hope you are now satisfied.'

'Yes, I am. Frankly, I was sorry for you, but not now. I am pleased that after putting up with my father for what must have seemed an interminable time, you have finally won through.'

Helga stared at her.

'I don't know what you mean.'

'You love all the trappings that go with money, don't you? There are very few women who could take on the role of Mrs. Herman Rolfe as well as you do. If anyone deserves my father's money and who can handle it as it should be handled, it's you. You've worked hard enough.'

This was so unexpected that Helga had to look away. Finally, steadying her voice, she said, 'Yes, I have worked for it, but I have also cheated. I have something here for you to read.' She drew the red folder from under her cushion and handed it to Terry.

The girl looked sharply at her, then opened the folder and took out Rolfe's letter.

'You want me to read this?'

'Yes, please.'

Helga got to her feet and wandered down to the swimming pool. Well, this is it, she thought, I've done the correct thing. I shall regret it, but at least, I can wear a brass halo.

After a while, she came back and sat down. Terry had put the red folder on the table.

They looked at each other.

'Congratulations,' Helga said. 'You can now buy your Guru a Rolls without the support of the people.'

'This is old hat.' Terry flicked the red folder. 'Dick read it and told me about it. That was when he was so un-educated he even suggested we married and he would get rid of you and share all my father's money with me.' She laughed. 'I soon put that right.'

Helga stared at her.

'So he was going to be a murderer as well as a thief and a blackmailer.'

'That's right. He is a primitive.' Terry smiled, shaking her head. 'That's why I find him so intriguing. All that is in the past.'

Helga gave up.

'Well, anyway, you are now a millionairess. How does it feel?'

Terry again shook her head.

'I am disappointed in you. I was under the impression you were highly intelligent. I wouldn't touch a dime of my father's money. If I could earn a million it just might give me a kick, but not otherwise.' She smiled. 'It would be fun to try, but of course, it will never happen. No ... I don't want the million.'

Regarding her, Helga realized with a sense of shock this girl meant what she was saying.

'If you don't want the money now, you may later. I will ask Winborn to put it in trust for you.'

'You will do nothing of the kind! Now listen to me!' Terry's eyes had turned angry. 'You were only married to my father for a few years. I had to live with him for twenty years. I loathed him. He was a mean, narrow minded, soulless machine with a sadistic streak in him that made him as ruthless as a dictator! He treated my mother shamefully. He hadn't a spark of kindness nor understanding in him. He made me sick to my stomach and I walked out on him as soon as my mother died. She was one of the old-fashioned fools who stick to their men no matter how they are treated. I call myself Terry Shields because I can't stand the sound of his name. I repeat: I would rather starve to death than take a dime of his rotten money!'

Shocked, Helga stared at her.

'But you can't . . .'

'Hear me out!' Terry's voice rose. 'I am only going to his funeral because I don't want to hurt Hinkle. He imagines in his kind, out-of-this-world way that I was fond of my father. Without Hinkle I don't think my mother nor I would have been able to endure the misery of living with Herman Rolfe. From what you have said, it seems you intend to give this letter to Winborn. If you do, then I am really and truly disappointed in you. This letter was written by a sadistic-ego-maniac! If you tell me you couldn't live with your conscience if you didn't obey his mean death wish, then I say you are trying to make a martyr of yourself and I assure you, you don't fit the rôle of a martyr. Remember this: the dead can't care. It is the living who matter.' She got to her feet. 'I hope very soon to be reading about the fabulous Mrs. Herman Rolfe doing fabulous things and having the time of her life.' She smiled: a wide, friendly smile. 'See you in church,' and turning, she walked across the patio and down to the beach.

Motionless, Helga watched her until she was out of sight.

'I overheard the last part of the conversation, madame,' Hinkle said as he came forward with a cocktail shaker and a glass on a tray. 'As I have already observed: a remarkable young person with character.' He placed the tray on the table and then poured the drink.

As Helga watched him, he picked up the red folder.

'As you won't be needing this, madame,' he said smoothly, 'I suggest I consign it to the incinerator.'

Helga reached for the drink.

'Your suggestions are always sound, Hinkle.'

'I like to think so, madame.' He paused. 'Perhaps an omelette for dinner?'

'That would be lovely.'

She watched him walk away, carrying the red folder and she relaxed back in her chair.

At last the magic key was hers!

THE END